Charles Sellers

Tales from the lands of nuts and grapes

Charles Sellers

Tales from the lands of nuts and grapes

ISBN/EAN: 9783337174729

Printed in Europe, USA, Canada, Australia, Japan

Cover: Foto ©Andreas Hilbeck / pixelio.de

More available books at **www.hansebooks.com**

tales

from the lands of

nuts and grapes

(SPANISH AND PORTUGUESE FOLKLORE)

BY

CHARLES SELLERS.

1888.

LONDON :

Field & Tuer, The Leadenhall Press, E.C.

Simpkin, Marshall & Co.; Hamilton, Adams & Co.

FIELD & TUER,
THE LEADENHALL PRESS, E.C.
(T. 4,355)

PREFACE.

I FIRMLY believe that the following tales have never seen the light of publicity. They are the folklore of Spain and Portugal.

Since the day when Hernando del Castillo, in 1511, published some of the romances of Spanish chivalry collected from the people, various works have appeared at different times, adding to the already rich store from that inexhaustible mine of song and story.

But, unfortunately for those who appreciate originality in a people, it was discovered that Boccaccio had been most unceremoniously plagiarized, and, what was still worse, that his defects had not been avoided.

The "Decameron" has, in fact, been the foundation of the majority of the romances attributed to the natives of the Peninsula when, as has too often been the case, they have in their songs of chivalry overstepped the limits imposed by decorum.

But this does not argue that the Spaniards and Portuguese have no poetry and no folklore of their own, but rather that the latter have been ignored by the compilers of such literature, in order to satisfy the cravings of the unfortunately too many admirers, even in this day, of that which would have been of advantage to the world at large had it never been imagined.

In England the tale of "Jack the Giant Killer" is read with avidity by all young people, for it is a purely national tale; but in Spain and Portugal such simple tales very seldom find a publisher, and children, and even their elders have to content themselves with hearing them recited by those who enliven the long wintry nights with such lore as I have attempted to reproduce from my memory, told me in my youth in the bosom of those two sister lands which produced the Cid Campeador and the Gran Vasco da Gama.

And, before closing this preface, I would remark that the North of Portugal, where I was born and bred, is richer in folklore than the rest of the kingdom, especially in tales about enchanted Moors and warlocks, of whom I, in common with the Portuguese, say, "Abernuncio."

C. SELLERS.

CONTENTS.

TALES FROM THE LANDS OF
NUTS AND GRAPES.

THE INGENIOUS STUDENT.

THERE was once a student in Tuy who was so very poor that, if faith in Providence be not reckoned, he possessed no riches.

But Juan Rivas was endowed with a wonderfully fine gift of ingenuity, and although he was somewhat behind in the payment for the Masses on behalf of his predecessors, and even more so with his mundane creditors, still was he a man who meant well and would do the right thing if he only had the opportunity.

To the man of the world there is no greater pleasure than to pay his debts, for by so doing he increases his credit.

Juan Rivas would willingly have paid every

creditor had his pocket been as full of the wherewithal as his heart was of gratitude for small mercies ; but there is no difficulty about showing one's self desirous of satisfying one's debts—the only difficulty generally rests in being able to do so.

At college he had proved himself a good scholar and a true companion ; but as he could no longer contribute toward the support of his college, his college could not be expected to support him.

His long black cap, his flowing robes, his pantaloons, and his shoes were altered in substance, and so was Juan Rivas.

Finally he became reduced to his last maravedi, and as his friends could no longer assist him, he thought it was high time he should assist himself.

" Providence," said he, " has never intended me for a poor man, but Fate has almost made me one. I will believe in Providence, and become rich from this day." Saying which, he went to some of his companions, who were almost as poor as he was, and asked them if they desired to be rich.

" Do you ask us if we want to be rich with so serious a face ? " answered they. " Really, friend Juan, you are so strange that you do not seem to belong to this city !"

" No man can be rich," continued Juan, "by staying at home. We are students, and our studies should meet with some recompense. Will you do as I bid you ?"

" Yes !" cried all his poor companions ; " so long as you lead us not to the gallows, for we like not such playthings."

" Well, then, follow me," said Juan ; "and when you see me release a prize that belongs to him who shall be bold enough to seize it, off with it to the market, and dispose of it at the best possible price.

" Done, and agreed to," shouted all, " if you will but seize the prize !"

" Leave that to me," said the poor student, "and I will hand you a prize fully worth twenty dollars without his garments."

" But, surely, you are not going to hand some man or woman over to us ?" inquired they.

" Ask me no questions, as the Archbishop of Compostella said to the pretty widow, and I will be honest with you. The prize I shall hand you will fetch money in the market, and we sell not human beings in this country," urged Juan.

" That is right," they exclaimed ; " and we will follow you."

The students followed Juan on to the high-road leading from the city to Ourense ; and when they had walked for about two hours' time Juan told his companions to get behind the hedge and await results.

Soon after, the jingling of bells was heard, and a muleteer seated cross-legged on a mule, which preceded five others, was seen approaching.

As the muleteer had sold all his wares he was indulging in a sleep, and had it not been for the dog-flies that teased the mules they would also have slept.

Juan let the muleteer pass ; but as the last mule came up he seized it, and, taking off its trappings, and disencumbering it of its ponderous albarda, or saddle, he freed the animal on the roadside, and replaced the trappings and the saddle on himself.

His companions were not slow in seizing the prize and hurrying away with it, while Juan Rivas continued for some distance along the road, following in the train of mules.

As soon as he considered that his companions would be out of sight, he commenced backing with all his strength, which brought the mules to a sudden halt and caused their bells to tinkle.

The muleteer looked back to see if anything was wrong, but, perceiving nothing, bestowed a hearty blow on his mule, and on he went again.

The student now began to rear and jump about so that the muleteer pulled up, and, having dismounted, proceeded to inquire into the cause of the mule so misbehaving itself; but his astonishment was great when, instead of a mule, he saw a human being bearing the trappings and the saddle.

"What merry freak is this," demanded the muleteer, addressing the student, "that I see you replacing my mule?"

"It is no merry freak, indeed it is not," replied Juan Rivas, "but a sad reality. You see before you, good master, a poor, miserable creature, who for his many offences against Mother Church was transformed into a mule, and sentenced to remain so for a number of years. My term of punishment has just expired, and I am restored to my natural form."

"But where is my mule that cost me one hundred crowns not many years ago?" asked the muleteer.

"You do not understand me, good master," replied the student. "I was the mule, and the mule was I; now I am I. When you used to kick your mule, you really kicked me; when you fed it, you fed me; and now, when you speak to me, you speak to all that remains of your mule. Now do you understand?"

"I am beginning to perceive," said the muleteer, scratching his head and looking very sorrowful, "that for your sins you were turned into a mule, and that for mine, I had the misfortune to purchase you. I always thought there was something strange about that mule!"

"There is no doubt that we all must put up with the consequences of our evil ways, and, as you very properly say, you have been punished by the loss of your mule; but, then, you can rejoice with me, seeing that the son of the first Grandee in Spain served you in the humble capacity of a beast of burden, and now is restored to rank and wealth."

"And are you a Grandee of Spain?" anxiously inquired the poor man, "Why, then, your excellency will never forgive me for the many kicks I have bestowed on your excellency's sides; and I am a ruined man, for you will have me punished."

" Not so, kind friend ; not so," replied the
student, in an assuring tone ; " for how could
you tell that your mule was not a mule ? "

" Then your excellency will not be revenged
on me ? " continued the muleteer. " And if it
will be of any consolation to your excellency,
I promise never to divulge this mystery ! "

" It will, indeed, be a great comfort to me
to think that no one will know what became of
me for so many years," replied the student.
" And now I must bid you good-bye, for I am
in a hurry to again embrace my dear parents if
they be still living."

" Good-bye," said the muleteer, with emotion ;
"and may your excellency never again incur
the displeasure of Mother Church."

Thus they parted good friends ; the muleteer
pondering over what he termed the mysteries
of life, and Juan Rivas full of delight at the
thought of rejoining his companions, and having
a good supper with the proceeds of the mule,
which pleasure was not denied him and his
friends.

In a fortnight's time there was a cattle fair
in the neighbourhood of Tuy, and as the muleteer required to replace the mule he had so
mysteriously lost, he attended the fair, and was

looking about him for a serviceable mule, when an acquaintance called out to him to know why he had parted with the other one.

" I have my private reasons," answered the muleteer, "and I am not here to let you know them."

" Very true," continued his inquisitive friend ; " but the proverb says that ' the mule you know is better than the mule you don't know,' and if you will take my advice, you will buy your old mule back again, for there it is "—pointing to it.

The muleteer looked in the direction mentioned, and was horrified at seeing his late mule again ; but, trying to conceal his emotion, he approached the animal and whispered in its ear, "Those who don't know what sort of a mule your excellency is may buy you, but I know the mule you are;" and, turning away, he sorrowfully exclaimed, " He has again offended. Terrible are the judgments of Providence ! "

THE UGLY PRINCESS.

THERE was once a king who had an only daughter, and she was so very ugly and deformed that, when she rode through the streets of Alcantara, the children ran away, thinking she was a witch.

Her father, however, thought her the most lovely creature in his kingdom; and as all the courtiers agreed with him, and the Court poet was always singing her praises, the princess had been led to believe what most ladies like to believe; and as she was expecting a prince from a distant country, who was coming expressly to marry her, she had ordered many rich dresses which only made her look uglier.

The city of Alcantara was ready to receive Prince Alanbam, who was going to espouse the Princess Altamira.

Crowds thronged the streets, martial music was heard everywhere, and in the public square

a splendid throne had been erected for the
king, Princess Altamira, and Prince Alanbam.

Around the throne were formed large bodies
of well-equipped cavalry, dark visaged warriors
clad in white and gold, and mounted on superb
Arab steeds.

Behind the king, on his left side, stood the
royal barber with his retinue of apprentices ;
and on his right side was seen Nabó the
headsman, a nigger of gigantic stature, with
his implement of office, an axe, over his
shoulder.

Seated on the steps of the throne were a
number of musicians, and below these a guard
of honour, composed of foot soldiers dressed in
short vests, called "aljubas," and wide lower
garments, and with their aljavas, or quivers,
full of bright arrows.

From the throne the king could see the
splendid bridge on six pillars, built by Trajan,
along which a brilliant cavalcade was proceeding, namely, the procession formed by Prince
Alanbam and his retainers.

As soon as the prince, after saluting the
king, beheld the princess, he turned pale, for
he had never seen any one so ugly ; and however much he might have desired to keep up

an appearance of courtesy to the princess before
her father's subjects, he could not kiss her as
she expected him to do, nor could he be per-
suaded to occupy the chair reserved for him
beside the princess.

"Your mercy," said he, addressing the king,
"must excuse my insuperable bashfulness; but
the fact is that the Princess Altamira is so
transcendently beautiful, and so dazzling to
behold, that I can never expect to look upon
her face again and live."

The king and the princess were highly
flattered; but as Prince Alanbam continued
obdurate in his professions of bashfulness, they
commenced to feel somewhat vexed, and at
last the king said in a loud voice—

"Prince Alanbam, we fully appreciate the
motive that prompts your conduct, but the
fact is the Princess Altamira is present to be
wedded to you; and, as a Christian king, the
first of my line, I desire to lead to the altar
my only daughter, Princess Altamira, and her
affianced husband, Prince Alanbam."

"It cannot be," said the prince. "I would
rather marry some one less beautiful. Sir
king, forgive me if I annoy you, but I will not
be wedded to so much beauty."

The king was now incensed beyond measure, and the princess his daughter, thinking to spite Prince Alanbam, said—

"With your permission, royal father, since I am too beautiful for a prince, I will be married to the most learned man in your kingdom— Bernardo, the royal barber."

"And that you shall," said the king ; but, on turning round to speak to the barber, he found that this the most learned man in his kingdom was all of a tremble, as if dancing to the music of St. Vitus.

"What has possessed thee, caitiff ? " asked the king. " Hearest not thou the honour that is to be conferred on thee ? "

" My royal master," muttered the poor frightened man of learning and lather, " I can no more avail myself of the honour which you would confer on me than the Archbishop of Villafranca could. His grace is bound to celibacy, and I am already married."

Now, the barber had on many occasions rendered himself obnoxious to Sanchez, the royal cobbler, who, seeing the king's perplexity, and a chance of avenging past insults, ex-claimed—

" Royal master, it would be most acceptable

to your subjects that so much beauty should be wedded to so much learning. Our good friend, Bernardo, was, it is true, married; but since he has been in attendance at the palace, he has so fallen in love with Princess Altamira that he no longer notices his wife; therefore, may it please your mercy to dissolve the first marriage, and announce this new one with her highness, your daughter ? "

The barber at this harangue became so infuriated that he rushed blindly at the cobbler, and with his razor would have severed his head from the rest of his body, but that he was prevented by the guard, who held him down.

"Executioner, do your work!" cried the baffled king; and at one blow the head of the unfortunate barber rolled on the ground.

Prince Alanbam seeing this, and fearing that more mischief might ensue, proposed to the king that one hundred knights should be chosen, and that these should fight for the hand of the lovely Princess Altamira. "I myself will enter the lists," said the prince; "and the survivor will be rewarded by marrying your daughter."

"That is a good idea," said the king; and calling together ninety-nine of his best knights, he bade them fight valiantly, for their reward was very precious.

Fifty knights, mounted on beautiful chargers, placed themselves on one side, and were opposed by forty-nine equally well-mounted knights and Prince Alanbam ; and at the word of command, given by the king, they advanced at headlong speed against each other ; but, much to the astonishment of the spectators, no knight was unhorsed ; rather did it seem that each knight did his utmost to get run through by his opponent.

At it they went again and again, but with the same result, for no man was hurt, although seeming to court death.

"We will alter the order of things," exclaimed the king. "The knight who is first wounded shall be the one to marry the princess."

This was no sooner said than the knights seemed to be possessed of a blind fury, and at the first charge nearly every knight was unhorsed and every one wounded, while the confusion and noise were awful. They were all accusing each other of being the first wounded ; so that, in utter despair, the king declared his daughter should be married to the

Church, enter a convent, and thus hide her transcendent beauty.

"No, father," exclaimed the ugly princess; "I will get a husband; and if in all the states of Spain no one be found worthy enough to be my husband, I will leave Spain for ever. There is a country where the day never dawns, and night is eternal. Thither will I go; for in the dark, as all cats are gray, so are all degrees of beauty brought to one common level. I now know that it is just as unfortunate to be too beautiful as it is to be very ugly."

Having delivered herself of this speech, Princess Altamira bade the king, her father, good-bye, and was on the point of leaving the royal presence, when the handsome figure of Felisberto, the blind fiddler, was seen to approach.

"Princess," exclaimed blind Felisberto, "to Spain nothing is denied. You speak of proceeding to the North, where the day never dawns, in search of a husband. You need but look at me to behold one to whom night and day, extreme ugliness and transcendent beauty, are alike; and since all are so bashful that they will not marry you, allow me, fair princess, to offer you my services as a husband.

In my world 'handsome is that handsome does.' "

The king was so pleased with the blind fiddler's speech that he immediately made him a Grandee of Spain, and acknowledged him as his son-in-law elect.

THE WOLF-CHILD.

IN the North of Portugal there are many sequestered spots where the enchanted Moors and the wizards meet when it is full moon. These places are generally situated among high rocks on the precipitous sides of the hills overlooking rivers; and when the wind is very boisterous their terrible screams and incantations can be distinctly heard by the peasantry inhabiting the neighbouring villages.

On such occasions the father of the family sets fire to a wisp of straw, and with it makes the sign of the cross around his house, which prevents these evil spirits from approaching. The other members of the family place a few extra lights before the image of the Virgin; and the horse-shoe nailed to the door completes the safety of the house.

But it will so happen that sometimes an enchanted Moor, with more cunning than honesty, will get through one of the windows on the birth of a child, and will brand the infant with the crescent on his shoulder or arm, in which case it is well known that the child, on certain nights, will be changed into a wolf.

The enchanted Moors have their castles and palaces under the ground or beneath the rivers, and they wander about the earth, seeing but not seen ; for they died unbaptized, and have, therefore, no rest in the grave.

They seem to have given preference to the North of Portugal, where they are held in great fear by the ignorant peasantry; and it has been observed that all such of the natives as have left their homes to study at the universities, on their return have never been visited by the enchanted Moors, as it is well known that they have a great respect for learning. In fact, one of the kings has said that until all his subjects were educated they would never get rid of the enchanted Moors and wizards.

In a village called Darque, on the banks of the Lima, there lived a farmer whose goodness and ignorance were only equalled by those of his wife. They were both young and robust, and were sufficiently well off to afford the luxury of beef once or twice a month. Their clothes were home-spun, and their hearts were homely. Beyond their landlord's grounds they had never stepped; but as he owned nearly the whole village, it is very evident that they knew something of this world of ours. They were both born and married on the estate, as their parents had been before them, and they were contented because they had never mixed with the world.

One day, when the farmer came home to have his midday meal of broth and maize-bread, he found his wife in bed with a new-born baby boy by her side, and he was so pleased that he spent his hour of rest looking at the child, so that his meal remained untasted on the table.

Kissing his wife and infant, and bidding her beware of evil eyes, he hurried out of the house back to his work; and so great was his joy at being a father that he did not feel hungry.

He was digging potatoes, and in his excitement had sent his hoe through some of them, which, however, he did not notice until he happened to strike one that was so hard that the steel of his hoe flashed.

Thinking it was a pebble, he stooped to pick it up, but was surprised to see that it was no longer there.

However, he went on working, when he struck another hard potato, and his hoe again flashed.

"Ah," said he, "the evil one has been sowing this field with stones, as he did in the days of good Saint Euphemia, our patroness." Saying which, he drew out the small crucifix from under his shirt, and the flinty potato disappeared; but he noticed that one of its eyes moved.

He thought no more of this untoward event, and went on hoeing until sunset, when, with the other labourers, he shouldered his hoe and prepared to go home.

Never had the distance seemed so great; but at last he found himself by his wife's bedside. She told him that while he was absent an old woman had called, asking for something to eat, and that as she seemed to have met with some accident, because there was blood running down her face, she invited her in, and told her she might eat what her husband had left untasted.

Sitting down at the table, the old woman

commenced eating without asking a blessing on the food ; and when she had finished she approached the bed, and, looking at the infant, she muttered some words and left the house hurriedly.

The husband and wife were very much afraid that the old woman was a witch ; but as the child went on growing and seemed well they gradually forgot their visitor.

The infant was baptized, and was named John ; and when he was old enough he was sent out to work to help his parents. All the labourers noticed that John could get through more work than any man, he was so strong and active ; but he was very silent.

The remarkable strength of the boy got to be so spoken about in the village that at last the wise woman, who was always consulted, said that there was no doubt but that John was a wolf-child ; and this having come to the ears of his parents, his body was carefully examined, and the mark of the crescent was found under his arm.

Nothing now remained to be done but to take John to the great wise woman of Arifana, and have him disenchanted.

The day had arrived for the parents to take

John with them to Arifana, but when they looked for him he could nowhere be found. They searched everywhere—down the well, in the river, in the forest—and made inquiries at all the villages, but in vain; John had disappeared.

Weeks went by without any sign of him; and the winter having set in, the wolves, through hunger, had become more undaunted in their attacks on the flocks and herds. The farmer, afraid of firing at them, lest he might shoot his son, had laid a trap; and one morning, to his delight, he saw that a very large wolf had been caught, which one of his fellow-labourers was cudgelling. Fearing it might be the lost wolf-child, he hastened to the spot, and prevented the wolf receiving more blows; but it was too late, apparently, to save the creature's life, for it lay motionless on the ground as if dead. Hurrying off for the wise woman of the village, she returned with him; and, close to the head of the wolf, she gathered some branches of the common pine-tree, and lighting them, as some were green and others dry, a volume of smoke arose like a tower, reaching to the top of a hill where lived some notorious enchanted Moors and wizards; so

that between the wolf and the said Moors the
distance was covered by a tunnel of smoke and
fire. Then the wise woman intoned the following words, closing her eyes, and bidding the
rest do so until she should tell them they might
open them :—

> " Spirit of the mighty wind
> That across the desert howls,
> Help us here to unbind
> All the spells of dreaded ghouls ;
> Through the path of smoke and fire
> Rising to the wizards' mound,
> Bid the cursèd mark retire
> From this creature on the ground ;
> Bid him take his shape again,
> Free him from the Crescent's power,
> May the holy Cross remain
> On his temple from this hour."

She now made the sign of the Cross over the
head of the wolf, and continued :—

> " River, winding to the west,
> Stay thy rippling current, stay,
> Jordan's stream thy tide has blest,
> Help us wash this stain away ;
> Bear it to the ocean wide,
> Back to Saracenic shore.
> Those who washed in thee have died
> But to live for evermore."

Then she sprinkled a few drops over the fire,

which caused a larger amount of smoke, and
exclaimed—

> " Hie thee, spirit, up through smoke,
>   Quenched by water and by fire ;
> Hie thee far from Christian folk,
>   To the wizard's home retire.
> Open wide your eyelids now,
>   All the smoke has curled away ;
> 'Neath the peaceful olive bough
>   Let us go, and let us pray."

Then they all rose, and the wolf was no
longer there. The fire had burned itself out,
and the stream was again running. In slow
procession they went to the olive grotto,
headed by the wise woman ; and, after praying, they returned to the house, where they
found, to their delight, John fast asleep in his
bed ; but his arms showed signs of bruises
which had been caused by the cudgelling he
had received when he was caught in the trap.

There were great rejoicings that day in the
village of Darque ; and no one was better
pleased than John at having regained his proper
shape.

He was never known to join in the inhuman
sport of hunting wolves for pleasure, because,
as he said, although they may not be wolf-
children, they do but obey an instinct which

was given them ; and to be kind-hearted is to obey a precept which was given us. And, owing to the introduction into Portugal of the Book in which this commandment is to be found, wolf-children have become scarcer, and the people wiser.

THE MAGIC MIRROR.

IT was proclaimed throughout the kingdom of Granada that the king had decided on marrying. The news was first told to the court barber, then to the night watchmen, and, in the third place, to the oldest woman in the city of Granada.

The barber told all his customers, who again told all their friends. The night watchmen in crying the hour proclaimed the news in a loud voice, so that all the maidens were kept awake by thinking of the news, and by day they were being constantly reminded by all the old dueñas that the king had resolved to marry.

After the news had become somewhat stale, the question was asked, "Who is the king going to marry?" To which the barber made reply, that probably "he would marry a woman."

" A woman !" exclaimed his hearers. " Why, what else could he marry ? "

" Not all women are worthy the name," answered the barber. " Some more resemble the unbaptized, of whom I say, *abernuncio.*"

" But what mean you, good friend ? " demanded his customers. " Is not the king to find a woman for wife in our land of Spain ? "

" He would," replied the barber, " with greater ease find the reverse ; but to find a woman worthy to be his wife I shall have great trouble."

" What, *you?*" exclaimed all of them. " What have you got to do with providing the king with a wife ? "

" I am under royal licence, remember," said he of the razor ; " for I am the only man in the kingdom permitted to rub the royal features. I am the possessor of the magic mirror also, into which if any woman not being thoroughly good shall look, the blemishes on her character will appear as so many spots on its surface."

" Is this one of the conditions ? " asked all.

" This is the sole condition," replied the barber, placing his thumbs in the armholes of his waistcoat and looking very wise.

"But is there no limit as to age?" they again inquired.

"Any woman from eighteen years upwards is eligible," said the possessor of the mirror.

"Then you will have every woman in Granada claiming the right to be queen!" all exclaimed.

"But, first of all, they will have to justify their claim, for I will not take any woman at her word. No; she will have to gaze into the mirror with me by her side," continued the barber.

The sole condition imposed on those who desired to become Queen of Granada was made known, and was much ridiculed, as may naturally be supposed; but, strange to say, no woman applied to the barber to have a look into the mirror.

Days and weeks went by, but the king was no nearer getting a wife. Some generous ladies would try and prevail on their lady friends to make the trial, but none seemed ambitious of the honour.

The king, be it known, was a very handsome man, and was beloved by all his subjects for his many virtues; therefore it was surprising that none of the lovely ladies who attended court should try to become his wife.

Many excuses and explanations were given. Some were already engaged to be married, others professed themselves too proud to enter the barber's shop, while others assured their friends that they had resolved on remaining single.

The latter seem to have been cleverer in their excuses, for it was soon observable that no man in Granada would marry, assigning as a reason for this that until the king was suited they would not think of marrying; though the real cause may have been due to the objection of the ladies to look into the mirror.

The fathers of families were much annoyed at the apparent want of female ambition in their daughters, while the mothers were strangely silent on the matter.

Every morning the king would ask the barber if any young lady had ventured on looking into the mirror; but the answer was always the same—that many watched his shop to see if others went there, but none had ventured in.

" Ah, Granada, Granada ! " exclaimed the king; " hast thou no daughter to offer thy king ? In this Alhambra did my predecessors enjoy the company of their wives; and am I to be denied this natural comfort ? "

"Royal master," said the barber, "in those days the magic mirror was unknown and not so much required. Men then only studied the arts, but now is science added to their studies."

"You mean, then," asked the king, "that an increase in knowledge has done no good ? "

"I mean more than that," continued the barber; "I mean that people are worse than they used to be."

"'God is great!' is what these walls proclaim ; to know is to be wise," urged the king.

"Not always, sir," said the barber; "for the majority of men and women in the present know too much and are not too wise, although some deem them wise for being cunning. There is as great a distance between wisdom and cunning as there is between the heavens and the earth."

"Barber," shouted the king, "thou shalt get me a wife bright as the day, pure as dew, and good as gold—one who shall not be afraid to look into thy magic mirror ! "

"Sir," replied the barber, "the only magic about my mirror is that which the evil consciences of the ladies of Granada conjure up. The simple shepherdess on the mountain side would brave the magic power of any mirror, strong in the consciousness of innocence; but would you marry such a lowly one?"

"Such a woman is worthy to be a queen, for she is a pearl without price," answered the king. "Go, bid her come here; and, in the presence of my assembled court, let the gentle shepherdess look into the mirror, after thou hast told her of the danger of so doing."

The barber was not long in bringing the shepherdess to court with him; and it having been proclaimed throughout the city that the trial was going to be made, the principal hall was soon filled with all the grand ladies and knights of the king's household.

When the shepherdess entered the royal presence she felt very shy at being surrounded by so much grandeur; but she knew enough about her own sex to understand that they inwardly considered her not quite so ugly as they audibly expressed her to be.

The king was very much pleased with her appearance, and received her very kindly, telling her that if she desired to be his wife she would have to gaze into the magic mirror, and if she had done aught which was not consistent with her maidenly character, the mirror would show as many stains on its surface as there might be blemishes on her heart.

"Sir," replied the maiden, "we are all sinners in the sight of God, they say; but I am a poor shepherdess, and surrounded by my flock. I have known what it is to be loved, for, when the sheep have perceived danger, they have come to me for protection. The wild flowers have been my only ornament, the sky almost my only roof, and God my truest and best friend. Therefore, I fear not to look into that magic mirror ; for although I have no ambition to become queen, yet am I not lacking in that pride which is born of the desire to be good."

Saying which, she walked up to the mirror and gazed into it, blushing slightly, perhaps at the sight of her own beauty, which before she had only seen portrayed in the still brook.

The court ladies surrounded her ; and when they saw that the magic mirror showed no stains on its surface, they snatched it from her, and exclaimed—

"There is no magic in it—a cheat has been put on us!"

But the king said—

"No, ladies ; you have only yourselves to thank. Had you been as innocent as this shepherdess, who is going to be my queen, you would not have dreaded looking into the mirror."

After the marriage the barber was heard to say, that as the magic mirror had now lost its virtue, who could tell but what this charm might be restored to Granada?

THE BLACK SLAVE.

THERE was once a princess who had a black man slave.

"Princess," said the black slave one day, " I know that you love the good Count of Yanno very much; but you cannot marry him, for he is already married. Why not, then, marry me?"

"I love, as you say, the Count of Yanno, and I know that he is married; but my father is a very powerful king, and he can render his marriage void. As for you," continued the princess, "I would rather marry the lowest born man of my own race than a nigger!"

"Remember, princess, for how many years I have been your true slave—how I used to look after you when you were a child. Did I not once save you from the fangs of a wolf?"

"You need not tell me," answered the princess, "that you love me as slaves love their superiors; but should you ever speak

again about marrying me, I will tell my royal
father."

" If you mention the love that slaves generally
have to their owners, I will not contradict you ;
but I think that sometimes masters are more
unworthy the love of their slaves than the
slaves are entitled to the love of their masters,"
said the slave.

"You belong to us by purchase or by in-
heritance," continued the princess, "and we do
not belong to you. The white man gains the
love of the lady of his choice by deeds of arms ;
he bears on his lance the banner embroidered
by his lady-love, and, as a true knight, he makes
verses in her honour."

"Chivalry, as you understand it, is to me
a fable ; for if one of your pale-faced knights
risk his life, it is on behalf of his family pride,
although he may mention his lady-love's name
with his dying breath ; but if a slave lay down
his life for his master or mistress, it is only
reckoned a part of his duty," urged the slave.

" I command you not to speak to me again
like this," said the princess, " or I will have you
severely punished."

The poor slave was very sorrowful when he
heard the princess, whom he loved so dearly,

threaten to have him punished. "Death is the leveller of all ranks and of all races," said he; "the dust of the dead white man and of the nigger are alike; in death, the king is no more than the beggar. I will run away from this palace and seek refuge in the northern provinces, where, if the climate be colder, they say the hearts of the people are warmer."

That very night did Mobarec—for that was the name of the slave—leave the palace of his lady-love, the beautiful banks of the Guadal-quivir, and his favourite orange-groves. During the daytime he hid in the caves on the mountain-sides, and as soon as night set in he would continue his journey.

When he had been travelling like this for some weeks, and as he was making his way through a dark forest, he saw a brilliant light in the distance; and as he was very hungry, he hoped that it might be from some house where he might get food and rest. As he walked on he discovered that the light was not from a house, but that it was caused by a large bonfire, around which some men and women were seated.

Fearing that he might be in the neighbour-hood of robbers, he took the precaution of approaching by hiding behind the trees; and when he got near enough to the group to see them plainly, he observed that close to the fire there was a very old woman standing with her arms over the fire, and holding a child which screamed as if it were being burned.

Mobarec thought that the child was going to be roasted, and did not know that what he saw was simply the act of disenchantment, which was being carried out by the wise woman of the village on a child born with the evil eye.

Approaching still nearer, he heard the crone mutter some words, which Mobarec imagined to be used in order to stifle the piteous cries of the child.

The crone suddenly commenced shrieking and jumping over the fire, while the men and women who surrounded her beat the air with big sticks, which is done when the evil one is supposed to be leaving the body of the child.

Just at this moment Mobarec happened to show himself from behind the tree, when he was immediately observed by the wise woman, who directed all eyes to him; and their horror can be easily imagined when it is said that

Mobaree was the first nigger who had ever visited the northern parts of Spain.

Mobaree, on perceiving that he was seen, thought he would smile, in order to show them that he was a friend; but this made him look all the more terrible by the glare of the fire, and, thinking that he was the evil one that had just left the body of the child, they first of all crossed themselves and then ran towards Mobaree with their bludgeons, who, without more ado, took to his feet and was soon lost in the darkness of the forest.

Having baffled his pursuers, Mobaree sat down to rest and to think over what he had seen.

" I suppose," said he to himself, " that these people were trying to make a king by burning a white child until he became black, for I could see that they were not going to eat it. I have been told that in some parts they will only have black kings, and I am certainly in one of these parts."

Musing over this idea for a long time, he at last fell asleep, and dreamt that he had arrived at a large city, where the people had crowded to meet him, and that he was placed on a magnificent throne, crowned king, and had married his dear princess.

Then he thought he was in a magnificent bed-chamber, and that the sheets of his bed were fringed with fine lace ; but purposing to raise the richly embroidered clothes a little higher, as he felt cold, he placed his hands on some stinging nettles, which made him wake and look around.

The day was already commencing ; the timid rabbit was lurking about the dew-spangled leaves ; the linnets were hopping about from branch to branch, and the wheels of some market carts were heard creaking in the distance.

Mobaree got up, and looking at himself in the waters of a passing stream, he was surprised to see that he had a golden crown on his head. It was, however, but the morning sun shining through the thick foliage above him.

" I was a slave last night," exclaimed Mobaree ; " this morning I am a king."

He noticed the direction from which the noise of the cart wheels proceeded, and hurrying thither, he soon came within sight of some people who were carrying their wares to market.

Mobaree gradually approached them, and,

seeing him advance, they dropped their baskets, and would have run away if fear had not deprived them of the power to do so.

"Be not afraid," said the nigger, "for I am your king. Hitherto you have had to work for the rich, but now the rich shall work for you. There shall be no poverty in my kingdom, no hunger, and no sorrow. Bad husbands shall take the place of the asses at the mills, and quarrelsome wives shall have a borough to themselves. Go," continued he, addressing the crowd, "and tell the inhabitants of the city that I am approaching."

"Long live the king!" shouted his hearers. "Long live the good king who will free us from our quarrelsome wives!" exclaimed the men; "And who will send our cruel husbands to replace the asses at the mills!" shrieked the women. "Long live the king who will banish poverty!" cried all together.

Having given vent to their enthusiasm, they hurried off to the city, and the good news soon spread that a new king was coming, and that they would all be rich.

Then they prepared a richly caparisoned white mule, with tinkling bells round its neck and a cloth of gold on its back, for the black king's use, and they went out in a body to meet him.

Having approached Mobarec, they prostrated themselves before him, and were at first very much afraid ; but hearing him address the mule in a grand speech, they rose and listened.

" Sir," said Mobarec to the mule, " I feel highly flattered by this ovation, and I confer on you here the post of principal minister, which you richly deserve for the sagacity you have shown in preserving silence when all want to make themselves heard. You will see that the poor are provided for, and that they provide for the wants of their king and his chosen ministers, of which you are the chief. People," exclaimed Mobarec, "behold your king and his minister ! And from this day forward let every man and woman in my kingdom strive to be as sure-footed, patient, and silent as this my minister."

It must be confessed that the people were somewhat surprised at the turn events had taken ; but as, recently, they had had a most unjust chief minister, they contented themselves with the knowledge that his successor could not introduce any cruel measures.

With similar ideas occupying them, they

retraced their way to the city, preceded by their black king and his chief minister.

Arrived at the palace, Mobarec entered and took his seat on the throne, his chief minister standing close to the lowest step. He then addressed the audience as follows—

"I make it known that the rich persons of this kingdom shall, if so required, give up their wealth to the poor, who will then become rich; but, as I would not that those who have hitherto been poor should forget their duty to their more unfortunate fellow-creatures, I declare that they shall have to contribute not only to the maintenance of the king, his ministers, and the state, but also to the requirements of those at whose expense they have themselves acquired riches. I also command that all disputes shall be submitted to the superior wisdom of my chief minister, without whose verbal consent it shall be treasonable to have recourse to blows; and I further require of my liege subjects that they engage in no war with neighbouring states without taking their wives to battle."

This speech was very much applauded, and the white mule, being unaccustomed to the surroundings, commenced braying so loudly

that Mobarec got up from his throne and
said—

" Listen to the voice of my minister ; he bids
you all be silent while you pay him homage."

Then one by one they passed before the
mule, bowing to him ; and when this ceremony
was finished Mobarec informed them that all
real kings were of his colour, but that he had
resolved on marrying the daughter of Xisto,
false king of Andalusia; and, therefore, he commanded twenty of his subjects to proceed to
that kingdom, and bring back with them the
fair Princess Zeyn, which was the name of the
princess he loved.

" If they ask you what I am like, say that
you have never seen one like me, and that my
wisdom is only approached by that of my chief
minister," said Mobarec.

At the end· of a month the twenty men
returned with the lovely princess, who, until
her marriage-day, was lodged in another
palace.

Great preparations were made for the occasion, excepting in one borough of the city,
which was deserted, for it had been assigned to
all quarrelsome wives.

The princess was naturally very anxious to

see her future husband, but etiquette forbade her doing so. Often had she thought of her runaway slave and lover. Absence had made her fonder of him, and little by little he had grown less black to her imagination.

At last the wedding-day arrived. Mobarec, attended by all his court, proceeded to the princess's palace, dressed in magnificent apparel, his strong black arms bare, but with splendid gold bracelets round them, and a belt of the same metal round his waist. His coat of mail was interwoven with threads of gold; but his heart required no gold to set it off, it was purity itself.

As soon as the princess saw him she recognized her former slave, and, hurrying to meet him, threw her arms round his neck, exclaiming—

"I am not worthy to marry so good a man; but if you will have me, I am yours."

"Princess," exclaimed Mobarec, "if I before was thy slave, I am none the less so now; for since the first man was created, beautiful woman has made all men captives. If I have aught to ask of thee now, 'tis that thy dominion over thy new subjects shall be as pleasant to them as it will be delightful to me."

From so wise a king and good a queen the people derived great benefit; disputes never went beyond the ears of the chief minister, and, in the words of the immortal barber and poet of the city, " the kingdom flourished under the guidance of a mule; which proves that there are qualities in the irrational beings which even wisest ministers would do well to imitate."

IT is a point of faith accepted by all devout
Portuguese that thirty-three baths in the
sea must be taken on or before the 24th of
August of every year. Although the motive
may not seem to be very reasonable, still the
result is of great advantage to those believers
who occupy thirty-three days in taking the
thirty-three baths, for otherwise the majority
of them would never undergo any form of
ablution.

That the demon is loose on the 24th of
August is an established fact among the credu-
lous ; and were it not for the compact entered
into between St. Bartholomew and the said
demon, that all who have taken thirty-three
baths during the year should be free from his
talons, the list of the condemned would be
much increased.

Now, there was a very powerful baron, whose

castle was erected on the eastern slope of the
Gaviarra, overlooking the neighbouring provinces of Spain, and he had always refused to
take these thirty-three baths, for he maintained
that it was cowardly on the part of a man
to show any fear of the demon. His castle
was fully manned; the drawbridge was never
left lowered; the turrets were never left un-
guarded; and a wide and deep ditch surrounded
the whole of his estates, which had been given
him by Affonso Henriques, after the complete
overthrow of the Saracens at Ourique, in
which famous and decisive battle the baron had
wrought wondrous deeds of bravery.

All round the castle were planted numerous
vines, which had been brought from Burgundy
by order of Count Henry, father of the first
Portuguese king; and in the month of August
the grapes are already well formed, but the
hand of Nature has not yet painted them.
Among the vines quantities of yellow melons
and green water-melons were strewn over the
ground, while the mottled pumpkins hung gracefully from the branches of the orange-trees.

In front of the castle was an arbour, formed
of box-trees, under which a lovely fountain had
been constructed; and here, in the hot summer

months, would wander the baron's only
daughter, Alina. She was possessed of all
the qualities, mental and physical, which went
towards making the daughter of a feudal lord
desired in marriage by all the gallants of the
day; and as she was heiress to large estates,
these would have been considered a sufficient
prize without the said qualities. But Alina, for
all this, was not happy, for she was enamoured of
a handsome chief, who, unfortunately, wore the
distinctive almexia, which proved him to be
a Moor, and, consequently, not a fit suitor for
the daughter of a Christian baron.

" My father," she would often soliloquize, " is
kind to me, and professes to be a Christian.
My lover, as a follower of the Prophet, hates
my father, but, as a man, he loves me. For
me he says he will do anything ; yet, when I
ask him to become a Christian, he answers me
that he will do so if I can prevail on my father
to so far conform with the Christian law as to
take the thirty-three baths ; and this my father
will not do. What am I to do ? He would
rather fight the demon than obey the saint."

One day, however, she resolved on telling
her father about her courtship with the young
chief, Al-Muli, and of the only condition he

made, on which depended his becoming a convert to Christianity, which so infuriated the baron that, in his anger, he declared himself willing to meet the demon in mortal combat, hoping thus to free the world of him and of the necessity of taking the thirty-three baths.

This so much distressed Alina, that when, during the afternoon of the same day, Al-Muli met her in the arbour, she disclosed to him her firm resolution of entering a convent, and spending the rest of her days there.

"This shall not be!" cried Al-Muli; and, seizing her round the waist, he lifted her on to his shoulder, sped through the baronial grounds, and, having waded through the ditch, placed her on the albarda of his horse and galloped away.

Alina was so frightened that she could not scream, and she silently resigned herself to her fate, trusting in the honour of her lover.

The alcazar, or palace, of Al-Muli was situated on the Spanish side of the frontier; and, as they approached the principal gate, the almocadem, or captain of the guard, hurried to receive his master, who instructed him to send word to his mother that he desired of her to receive and look after Alina. This done, he

E

assisted his bride elect to dismount, and, with a veil hiding her lovely features, she was ushered by Al-Muli's mother into a magnificently furnished room, and took a seat on a richly embroidered cushion, called an almofada.

To her future mother-in-law she related all that referred to her conversation with her father, and how she had been brought away from his castle ; and she further said that she very much feared the baron would summon all his numerous followers to rescue her.

Al-Muli's mother was a descendant of the Moors who first landed at Algeziras, and from them had descended to her that knowledge of the black art which has been peculiar to that race. She, therefore, replied that although she could count on the resistance her almogavares, or garrison soldiers, would offer to the forces of the baron, still she would do her utmost to avoid a conflict. She then proceeded to another room, in which she kept her magic mirror, and having closed the door, we must leave her consulting the oracle.

The baron was not long in discovering the absence of his daughter, and he so stormed about the place that his servants were afraid to come near him.

In a short time, however, his reason seemed to return to him, and he sat down on his old chair and gave way to grief when he saw that his Alina's cushion was vacant.

"My child—my only child and love," sobbed the old man, "thou hast left thy father's castle, and gone with the accursed Moor into the hostile land of Spain. Oh, that I had been a good Christian, and looked after my daughter better! I have braved the orders of good St. Bartholomew; I would not take the thirty-three baths in the sea, and now I am wretched!"

The baron suddenly became aware of the presence of a distinguished and patriarchal looking stranger, who addressed him thus—

"You mortals only think of St. Barbara when it thunders. Now that the storm of sorrow has burst on you, you reproach yourself for not having thought of me and of my instructions. But I see that you are penitent, and if you will do as I tell you, you will regain your daughter."

It was St. Bartholomew himself who was speaking, and the baron, for the first time in his life, shook in his shoes with fear and shame.

"Reverend saint," at last ejaculated the baron,

"help me in this my hour of need, and I will promise you anything—and, what is more, I will keep my promises."

" And you had better do so," continued the saint; " for not even Satan has dared to break his compact with me. You don't know how terrible I can be!"—here the saint raised his voice to such a pitch that the castle shook. " Only let me catch you playing false with me, and I'll—I'll—I don't know what I'll do!"

" Most reverend saint and father, you have only to command me and I will obey," murmured the affrighted baron—" I will indeed. Good venerable St. Bartholomew, only give me back my daughter—that is all I ask."

" Your daughter is now in the hands of Al-Muli, her lover, who dwells in a stronger castle than yours, and who, moreover, has a mother versed in the black art. It is no good your trying to regain her by the force at your disposal; you must rely on me—only on me. Do you understand?" asked the saint.

" Yes, dear, good, noble, and venerable saint, I do understand you; but what am I to do?"

" Simply follow me, and say not a word as you go," commanded the patriarch.

The baron did as he was told; and out from

the castle the two went unseen by any one.
The baron soon perceived that he was hurrying
through the air, and he was so afraid of falling
that he closed his eyes. All at once he felt
that his feet were touching the ground; and,
looking around him, what was his delight
to find himself close to his dear daughter
Alina.

"Father—dear father!" exclaimed Alina;
"how did you come here so quickly, for I
have only just arrived? And how did you
pass by the guards?"

The baron was going to tell her, but the
saint, in a whisper, enjoined silence on this
point; and the baron now noticed that the
saint was invisible.

"Never mind, dear child, how I came here;
it is enough that I am here," replied her father.
"And I intend taking you home with me, dear
Alina. The castle is so lonely without you;"
and the old man sobbed.

At this moment Al-muli entered the chamber,
and, seeing Alina's father there, he thought
there had been treachery among his guards; so
striking a gong that was near him, a number of
armed men rushed in.

"How now, traitors!" said he. "How have

you been careful of your duties when you have allowed this stranger to enter unobserved ? "

The soldiers protested their innocence, until at last Al-muli commenced to think that there must be some secret entrance into his castle.

" Search everywhere ! " screamed the infuriated Moor. " Have the guard doubled at all the entrances, and send me up the captain ! "

Al-muli's instructions were carried out, and the captain reported that all was safe.

" Old man," said the Moor, addressing the baron, " I have thee now in my power. Thou wert the enemy of my noble race. To thy blind rage my predecessors owed their downfall in Portugal. Thy bitter hatred carried thee to acts of vengeance. Thou art now in my power, but I will not harm one of thy grey hairs."

" Moor," replied the baron, with a proud look, " can the waters of the Manzanares and of the Guadalquivir join ? No ! And so cannot and may not thy accursed race join with ours ! Thy race conquered our people, and in rising against thine we did but despoil the despoiler."

" Thy logic is as baseless as thy fury was wont to be," answered the Moor. " Though hundreds of miles separate the Manzanares from the Guadalquivir, yet do they meet in the mightier waters of the ocean. Hadst thou said that ignorance cannot join hands with learning, thou wouldst have been nearer the mark, or that the Cross can never dim the light of the Crescent."

These words were spoken in a haughty manner; and as Al-muli turned round and looked upon his splendidly arrayed soldiers, who surrounded the chamber, his pride seemed justified.

"Thou canst not crush me more than thou hast done, vile Moor," said the baron. "Thou hast robbed me of my daughter, not by force of arms, but stealthily, as a thief at midnight. If any spark of chivalry warmed thy infidel blood thou wouldst blush for the act thou hast wrought. But I fear thee not, proud Moor; thy warriors are no braver than thy women. Dare them to move, and I will lay thee at my feet."

"Oh, my father, and thou, dear Al-Muli, abandon these threats, even if you cannot be friends."

"No, maiden," exclaimed Al-Muli; "I will not be bearded in my own den. Advance, guards, and take this old man to a place of safety below!"

But not a soldier moved ; and when Al-Muli was about to approach them to see what was the matter with them, his scimitar dropped from his hand, and he fell on the ground.

" What charm hast thou brought to bear on me, bold baron," screamed the Moor, "that I am thus rendered powerless ? Alina, if thou lovest me, give me but that goblet full of water, for I am faint."

Alina would have done as her lover bade her, but just then the figure of the venerable St. Bartholomew was seen with the cross in his right hand.

" Moor and infidel," said the saint, " thou hast mocked at this symbol of Christianity, and thou hast done grievous injury to this Christian baron ; but thou hast been conscientious in thy infidelity. Nor am I slow to recognize in thy race a knowledge of the arts and sciences not yet extended to the Christian. Yet, for all this, thou art but an infidel. Let me but baptize thee with the water thou wouldst have drunk, and all will yet be well."

" No, sir saint," answered the Moor. "When in my castle strangers thus treat me rudely, I can die, but not bend to their orders. If yonder baron is a true Christian, why has he not taken the thirty-three baths enjoined by thee?"

"And if my father do take them, wilt thou, as thou didst promise me," said Alina, "be converted to the true faith?"

"The Moor breaks not his promise. As the golondrina returns to its nest in due season, so the man of honour returns to his promise." Then, turning to the baron, he demanded to know if he would comply with the saint's instructions.

"Yes," answered the baron; "I have promised the good saint everything, and I will fulfil my promises. Al-Muli, if you love my daughter, love her faith also, and I will then have regained not only a daughter, but a son in my old age."

"The promise of the Moor is sacred," said Al-Muli. "Baptize me and my household; and do thou, good baron, intercede for me with the venerable saint, for I like not this lowly posture."

"My dear Al-Muli," sobbed Alina for joy, "the Cross and the Crescent are thus united in the mightier ocean of love and goodwill. May the two races whom one God has made be reconciled! And to-morrow's sun must not set before we all comply with the condition imposed by St. Bartholomew."

The saint was rejoiced with the work he had that day done, and declared that the churches he liked men to construct are those built within them, where the incense offered is prayer, and the work done, love. "As for the baths, they are but desirable auxiliaries," said he.

THE WHITE CAT OF ECIJA.

FROM the gates of the palace, situated on a gentle eminence in the vicinity of Ecija, down to the banks of the Genil, the ground was covered with olive-trees ; and the wild aloes formed a natural and strong fence around the property of the White Cat of Ecija, whose origin, dating back to the days of Saracenic rule, was unknown to the liberated Spaniard.

There was a great mystery attaching to the palace and its occupants ; and although the servants of the White Cat were to all appearances human beings, still, as they were deaf and dumb, and would not, or could not, understand signs, the neighbours had not been able to discover the secret or mystery.

The palace was a noble building, after the style of the alcazar at Toledo, but not so large ; and the garden at the rear was laid out with many small lakes, round which, at short distances, stood beautifully sculptured statues of young men and women, who seemed to be looking sorrowfully into the water. Only the brain and hand of an exceptionally gifted artist could have so approached perfection as to make the statues look as if alive. At night strings of small lamps were hung round the lakes, and from the interior of the palace proceeded strains of sweet, but very sad music.

Curiosity had long ceased to trouble the neighbours as to the mysterious White Cat and her household, and, with the exception of crossing themselves when they passed by the grounds, they had given up the affair as incomprehensible.

Those, however, who had seen the White Cat, said that she was a beautiful creature ; her coat was like velvet, and her eyes were like pearls.

One day a knight in armour, and mounted on a coal-black charger, arrived at the principal hostelry in Ecija, and on his shield he bore for his coat of arms a white cat rampant, and, underneath, the device, " Invincible."

Having partaken of some slight repast, he put spurs to his horse and galloped in the direction of the palace of the White Cat; but as he was not seen to return through the town, the people supposed that he had left by some other road.

The White Cat was seen next day walking about in the grounds, but she seemed more sorrowful than usual.

In another month's time there came another knight fully equipped, and mounted on a grey charger. On his shield he also displayed a white cat, with the device, " I win or die." He also galloped off to the palace, or alcazar, and was not seen to return ; but next day the White Cat was still more sorrowful.

In another month a fresh knight appeared. He was a handsome youth, and his bearing was so manly that a crowd collected. He was fully equipped, but on his shield he displayed a simple red cross. He partook of some food, and then cantered out of the town with his lance at rest. He was seen to approach the palace, and as soon as he thrust open the gate with his lance, a terrific roar was heard, and then a sheet of fire flashed from the palace door, and they saw a horrid dragon, whose long tail, as it lashed the air, produced such a wind that it seemed as if a gale had suddenly sprung up.

But the gallant knight was not daunted, and eagerly scanned the dragon as if to see where he might strike him.

Suddenly it was seen that the dragon held the White Cat under its talons, so that the Knight of the Cross in charging the dragon had to take care not to strike her. Spurring his horse on, he never pulled up till he had transfixed the dragon with his lance, and, jumping off the saddle, he drew his sword and cut off the monster's head.

No sooner had he done this than he was surrounded by ten enormous serpents, who tried to coil round him; but as fast as they attacked him, he strangled them.

Then the serpents turned into twenty black vultures with fiery beaks, and they tried to pick out his eyes; but with his trusty blade he kept them off, and one by one he killed them all, and then found himself surrounded by forty dark-haired and dark-eyed lovely maidens, who would have thrown their arms around him, but that he, fearing their intentions were evil, kept them off; when, looking on the ground, he saw the White Cat panting, and heard her bid him "strike."

He waited no longer, but struck at them and

cut off their heads, and then saw that the ground was covered with burning coal, which would have scorched the White Cat and killed her, had not the gallant knight raised her in his arms. He then placed her on his shield, and as soon as she touched the cross she was seen to change into a beautiful maiden, and all the statues round the lakes left their positions and approached her.

As soon as she could recover herself sufficiently to speak, she addressed the knight as follows—

"Gallant sir, I am Mizpah, only daughter of Mudi Ben Raschid, who was governor of this province for many years under the Moorish king, Almandazar the Superb. My mother was daughter of Alcharan, governor of Mazagan, and she was a good wife and kind mother. But my father discovering that she had forsaken the faith of her fathers, and had embraced the religion of the Cross, so worried her to return to her childhood's faith that she died broken-hearted. Then he married again, and his second wife, my stepmother, was a very wicked woman. She knew that I was a Christian at heart, and that my lover was also a Christian; so one day, when my father

was holding a banquet, she said to him, ' Mudi
Ben Raschid, the crescent of the Holy Prophet
is waning in thy family—thy daughter is a
renegade!'

"Then he was very much annoyed, and exclaimed that he would his palace and his riches
were made over to the enemy of mankind and
I turned into a cat, than that so great a stain
should fall on his family. No sooner had he
finished speaking than he fell dead and his
wicked wife also, and I was turned into a cat;
my lover, Haroun, and all my young friends
were turned into stone, and my servants were
stricken deaf and dumb. Many a brave knight
has been here to try and deliver me ; but they
all failed, because they only trusted in themselves, and were therefore defeated. But thou,
gallant knight, didst trust more on the Cross
than on thyself, and thou hast freed me. I
am, therefore, the prize of thy good sword ;
deal with me as thou wilt."

The Knight of the Cross assured her that
he came from Compostella, where it was considered a duty to rescue maidens in distress,
and that the highest reward coveted was that
of doing their duty. He had in various parts
of the world been fortunate enough in freeing

others, and he had still more work before him. He trusted that the lovely Mizpah might long be spared to Haroun, and, saluting her, he galloped off.

Then was the wedding held, at which all the people from Ecija attended ; and the bridegroom, rising, wished prosperity to the good knight, St. James of Compostella, who had been the means of bringing about so much happiness.

THE CHURCH AUCTIONEER AND CLOWN OF VILLAR.

DOWN the slopes of the neighbouring mountains were heard the stirring sounds of the bagpipes and drums, and at short intervals a halfpenny rocket would explode in mid-air, streaking the blue sky with a wreath of smoke.

Nearer and nearer came the sounds, and the villagers stood at their cottage doors waiting for the musicians to pass. Next to the firing of rockets nothing can be more heart-stirring than the martial sound of the pipes and drums. The big drum was, on this occasion, played most masterly by the auctioneer and clown of the parish church, called José Carcunda, or Joseph the Hunchback.

José Carcunda was dressed in his gala uniform—cocked hat, scarlet coat with rich gold lace embroidery, white trousers, and red

morocco slippers. He was a clever man, and
could take many parts in the church plays acted
in public for the benefit of the faithful. Sometimes he was Herod, at others, St. Joseph;
again he would appear as Judas, and then as
Solomon; but in this latter capacity he had
given some offence to the vicar by appearing
on the stage under the influence of drink.

Of all the weaknesses to which human flesh
is heir, none is more despised in Portugal than
drunkenness. Wine is emblematical of that
stream which flowed from the Crucified on
Calvary, and the abuse of such a precious gift
is not easily overlooked.

Within the narrow bounds of their primitive
way of thinking are cast some of the finest
traits in the character of the Portuguese
peasantry, although, in many instances, to this
very same source must be attributed some of
their peculiar ideas as to fate. They are
fatalists to a very great extent.

In Roman Catholic countries, the Sabbath
is remembered by attending mass in the
morning, and by amusements in the afternoon.
No public-house, with its glittering lights within, ·
with its bright and cosy fire, and with its
grand display of mirrors and pictures, invites

the peasant to step inside and gossip about his neighbours, while sipping the genial juice of the grape, or the *fire-water* that gives to the eye a supernatural brightness, and to the tongue a rush of foolish language. There is no law against such houses, but there is a popular prejudice.

José Carcunda was heard to say, after he had been guilty of drinking to excess when attired as Solomon, that his faithful dog Ponto refused to accompany him home on that occasion; "And as the creature stared at me," said he, "I could see shame and sorrow mingling in his eyes."

"There comes the Carcunda!" exclaimed the village belle, Belmira. "He is half hidden by the drum; but to-morrow we shall see him at early mass, when the good St. Anthony is to be raised to the rank of major."

"Yes," said her lover, Manoel; "and it will be a grand sight, for the priest showed me the *Gazette* in which is the king's warrant. St. Anthony's regiment is to arrive to-morrow, and after the image has donned the uniform the soldiers will present arms, the bombs will explode, rockets will be fired, and the band will play."

As the musicians entered the village, heralding the grand entertainment to be held next day, the people cheered them heartily, and followed them to the church, situated on the top of a small hill, around which bonfires were in course of preparation for the night.

A cart laden with water-melons, another with a pipe of green wine, and a few stalls where sweetstuff was exposed for sale, formed the principal feature of the fair.

The door of the church was thrown open, and the main altar was lit up with many lights. The chapels on each side were festooned with garlands of flowers; but that dedicated to the miraculous St. Anthony, junior major in the 10th regiment of infantry, was the grandest of all, with its magnificent silk draperies, and the altar decorated with flowers.

José Carcunda was a proud man that day. He had presided over all the arrangements, and they had given great satisfaction. Belmira had set the other girls the example of showing him their gratitude by kissing him. He was so overwhelmed by their caresses that he tried to get clear of them, lest his wife might be jealous; but it was of no use trying to free himself, for they made him sit on a stone bench, and, handing him a guitar, requested him to extemporize some verses :—

> " Fair ladies mine, I love the wine,
>   But music I love better;
> Still stronger far than song divine,
>   I love the ladies better.

> " I love the fields with flowerets bright,
>   The birds with carol merry;
> I love the——"

" No, I cannot sing just now; I am too happy," exclaimed the hunchback. " I feel like the rich miser of Santillana, when he recollected that he would be buried at the expense of the parish. So as my helpmate Joanna come not here, I care not how long the troops delay in arriving. Ah, Joanna is too good for me, as the runaway criminal said of the gallows; and the older she gets the more I recognize it! Yes, Joanna is too good for me and for this world; but we don't make ourselves—no, we don't do that."

Here José Carcunda shook his head very wisely, and looked at his slippered feet with some pardonable pride.

" Look you here," said one of his fair companions, " you are very stupid to-day; you will not sing, nor will you dance. Will you, then, tell us the tale about the sorrowful mule, and what befell her, or about the merry friar who turned highwayman to enrich the Church, or about the palaces of the enchanted Moors?"

"I will tell you something that happened to me when I was a young man," answered the hunchback.

"Know, then," continued José Carcunda, "that in my younger days I was an almocreve (muleteer), and owned six of the finest mules in the province of the Beira. I used to attend the weekly fair held at the university city, Coimbra, where I found a good market for my earthenware with which I loaded the mules.

"Fortune had favoured me, and I had saved some gold crowns; and on Sundays, when I had shaved and put on clean linen, I was the pride of the village.

"One summer's day, as I was leading my six mules, fully laden with pots and pans, to Coimbra, a student, who was on the roadside, saluted me and said—

"'Good José, I have a great favour to ask of you, and one that I know you will not deny me.'

"'Your excellency,' said I, 'has but to order,

and I will obey, so long as you place not my eternal happiness in jeopardy.'

"'The saints forbid,' answered the student, 'that I should ask you to do anything but what a Christian man should do! No, friend José, my errand is indeed a strange and sad one; but I feel that I must be as true to (with your leave) a mule as my profession requires me to be to a human being.'

"'What!' exclaimed I, 'are you under some spell, some wicked enchantment, that you make promises to (with your excellency's leave) a mule, which is the accursed animal since the days of Bethlehem?'

"'No, good friend,' continued the sorrowful student; 'I am under no spell, but under a vow; for I have promised to convey some sad news to (with your leave) that mouse-coloured mule of yours, and I feel that I must break it gently to her.'

"'Sir,' said I, 'you see before you a man who knows not the difference between the *Credo* and the *Paternoster* when they are written; and though I have heard say that if you want to see thieves you must get inside a prison and look at the passers-by, still am I not inclined to think that if you desire to see

knaves you must look in at the windows of the
university. My mule (with your excellency's
permission) is but a mule, and has no knowledge of sorrow or of language ; therefore, of
what avail to speak to her ? '

" ' You are much mistaken,' answered the
student, who now had tears in his eyes, ' for it
is well known that even the irrational animals
have feelings, and they have been heard to
speak. Good friend, grant me my request, for,
as I said before, I am under a vow.'

" ' Have your way, dear sir,' said I ; ' but if
the animal bites you, blame not me. She is
but a stubborn thing at the best of times.'

" The six mules were tied one to the other,
and each had a big load of pots and pans.
They were standing in the middle of the road
with their gay trappings and bells about them ;
and as I looked at the mouse-coloured one, I
wondered what the student could have to say
to her and how he would say it ; but, as you
know, these men who frequent the university
are so learned that they can repeat the *Credo*
backwards way, which is the great secret in the
black art.

" The student, having obtained my permission to speak to the mouse-coloured mule,

approached her gradually, exclaiming at intervals, 'Poor creature, how she will take it to heart! But I am under a vow. I must tell her—I must; but it is so painful!'

"'Senhor,' I exclaimed, 'you remind me of the Alcaide of Montijo, who hesitated to approach his mother-in-law until she was gloved. What you have to say, that say, and let me go my way.'

"'Unthoughtful man!' cried the student; 'little you wot of the sad news I have to break to that poor creature! To you a mule is but a four-legged creature, the cathedral bell but a thing of brass, and the university but the abode of the black art. You are absolutely ignorant, sir,' continued the student, 'for which you have much to be thankful; for if you were a student you would not sell earthenware pans, and would therefore lose the profit which you now make; and were you a student, you would at this moment be all of a tremble, for you would then know that we are at this present moment standing over a frightful abyss that will soon yawn to receive its prey.'

"I was now terribly frightened lest the student, in his calculations, should have made the mistake of a minute, so I rushed to the foremost mule so as to get her to lead the way out of the danger; but the student prevented me, saying—

" 'Not that way, for you will fall into the pit. Let me first of all whisper my news into the mouse-coloured mule's ear, and all may yet be well.'

" 'Hurry, then,' said I, 'or else we shall all be lost.'

" 'It is a very good thing to be in a hurry when you know what to do,' answered the student; 'but we must be cautious. Therefore, step lightly that way until you reach yonder lofty tree and get up it; but, before doing so, fill your pockets with stones.'

" I can assure you that I was not long in carrying out the student's instructions, and never have I trod so lightly on the ground as I did that day. The student, as soon as he saw me half-way up the tree, shouted out, 'Here it comes! Oh, this is awful—just as I told her all about it! Oh dear, oh dear!'

" I now noticed that the student was taking long jumps in the direction of the tree up which I had climbed, and at every jump he would call out, 'Shut your eyes, or you will become blind!'

"Then I heard a most dreadful noise, as if the end of the world had come; but I could still hear the student crying out, 'Shut your eyes, good friend, or you will be blinded!'

"I have never been so terrified either before or since that day, and I was also in considerable pain, as the stones which I had placed in the pockets of my pants had, with climbing, almost sunk into me.

"After having kept my eyes closed for some time, I ventured on opening them, and then I saw a sight which told me I was a ruined man. My mules were rolling about in the dust, and all my pots and pans were wrecked. The mouse-coloured mule, moreover, seemed to be demented; she rolled and writhed so that it seemed as if she were in awful distress, and there was no doubt but that she had dragged the others down with her.

"Suddenly I heard the voice of the student, and, looking down, I saw that he was seated on a branch just below me. 'Ah, poor creature,' said he, 'how terribly she feels the bereavement! Let us descend,' continued he, 'for the danger is now over, and we must, as Christian men, render aid to the poor dumb animals.' Saying which he slid down the tree, and I after

him as well as I could; and as soon as we again
got on the road, he bid me try to pacify the
mouse-coloured mule, while he would do his
utmost to get the leader to get up.

"I saw that all my earthenware was broken,
and I gave myself up to grief. 'Unlucky man
that I am!' I exclaimed. 'What harm can I
have done to have deserved so great a punishment, and what, sir student, did you say to yon
mule to make her act so?'

"'Alas, friend José,' said he, 'we of the
educated class understand resignation, but to
such as you, as well as to the irrational creation,
is this virtue denied. You bemoan the loss of
your earthenware; and yonder dumb creature,
with perhaps a glimmering of humanity about
her, but certainly with more reason than you,
deplores the loss of a good and beloved parent,
who, on his death-bed, implored me to inform
his daughter when I should next see her that
he had died thinking of her, and that he
bequeathed to her all he had to give, namely,
the right of pasturage over all the lands in Spain
and Portugal, and as much more as she could
snatch from her neighbour when in the stable.
Good-bye, friend José; my vow is accomplished,
and I leave you in peace with your mules.'

" ' And with the broken earthenware,' said I, 'and with my fortunes blasted, and with my legs bleeding ; and all because I met you ! '

" ' Say not so, friend José, for had it not been for me you would most assuredly have been swallowed up by the underground abyss. No, say not so, nor yet complain of your mouse-coloured mule, for to lament the death of a father is but natural.'

" The student walked quietly away, and I then set to making the mules get up, which, after much trouble, I succeeded in doing ; but noticing that the mouse-coloured mule kept her head on one side as if in pain, I examined her, and on looking into her ear I discovered the end of a cigarette which that vile student had purposely dropped into it.   I now knew that I had been deceived ; but the cheat had already disappeared, so, like a wise man, I trudged home, sold my animals to pay my debts, and, having nothing better to do, I married Joanna and became, as you know, the church clown and auctioneer."

THE WISE KING OF LEON.

THERE was a rich nobleman who had three sons ; and the king, being very fond of him, appointed the eldest son his page, the second his butler, and the youngest his barber.

The barber fell in love with the king's only daughter, who was equally fond of him ; and when this came to the ears of the king, he decided on putting a stop to it ; so he called for the princess, and said—

"I know that you are in love with my barber, and if you insist on marrying him I will have you killed."

The princess, on hearing her father say this, became very sorrowful, and asked him to allow her one day for consideration, to which the king acceded.

She then went to her room, and getting together some of her finest dresses, she made them up into a bundle, and left the palace by a secret door.

For seven days and nights did the princess walk through the forest, subsisting on wild fruit and the water from the rivulets. For seven days and nights did her father seek for her, and, not finding her, he sent for the barber, and told him that he must immediately go in search of the princess, and if he did not bring her back within a year he should die.

At the end of the seventh day the princess was so tired that she could not continue her journey; and being afraid of the wolves, she managed to climb on to the first branch of a large oak-tree; and when there, discovering that the trunk was hollow, she let herself slip down into the hollow, and there rested.

She had not been long in her hiding-place when her lover, the barber, approached, sighing, and saying to himself—

"Woe is me, for I shall never find the princess! There are so many lovely damsels in Castille, and yet I must fall in love with the king's only daughter."

The princess, hearing him speak, said in a disguised voice—

"Woe is the king's daughter! There are

so many gallants in Spain, and yet she must fall in love with her father's barber!"

The barber was much surprised to hear this apt rejoinder; but he could not find out from whence the voice came. He looked about everywhere, and at last, feeling sleepy, he lay down under the oak-tree where the princess was hidden.

In a very short time the barber was fast asleep; and the princess, hearing him breathe heavily, got out of her hiding-place, mounted the barber's horse, which the king had given him, and rode away with the barber's bundle of clothes, leaving her own in its place.

When she had ridden at full speed for some hours she dismounted, and opening the barber's bundle, she then disrobed herself and put on male attire.

Next day she had arrived in the kingdom of Leon, and she rode up to the king's palace and offered her services to the king as barber.

The king, being much struck by the stately bearing of the stranger, willingly accepted the proffered services.

When the real barber awoke and found his horse and clothes gone he was much alarmed; but seeing a bundle close to him he opened it,

G

and was delighted to find his lover's dresses in it.

Being a beardless youth, and very handsome, he bethought him of putting on the princess's finest dress; and as his hair was very long and curly, according to the fashion of the day, he made a very pretty woman.

Foot-sore and weary, he at last arrived at the palace of the King of Leon, and was admitted to the king's presence as the daughter of the neighbouring King of Castille.

The King of Leon was so charmed with the beauty of the new arrival that he could not sleep, and so he sent for the barber, to whom he confided his love.

The real princess was much astonished to hear that her lover was in the palace, for she guessed it was he in female attire; but she kept quiet until her lover was asleep in bed, and then she stole into his room, put back his clothes, and took her own away.

Next morning when the real barber awoke and found his magnificent dresses gone and his male attire restored to him he was indeed surprised; but there was no help for it—he must again become a man and a barber.

The princess put on her own clothes, and

hid in a cupboard of the room. When she saw her lover leave the room, and heard him go down the staircase, she closed the door behind him and finished her toilet.

The king got up earlier than usual, for he was so anxious to see the new arrival; but before doing so he sent for the barber to shave him.

They looked everywhere for him, but without success; and at last, in despair, they went to the bedroom of the new arrival, and, knocking at the door, intimated the king's command that she should present herself.

The princess was ready; and, slipping past the courtiers, presented herself before the king.

" Who are you ? " inquired the king.

" I am the daughter of the King of Castille, as I informed your mercy yesterday." answered the princess.

" But where, then, is my barber ? " rejoined the king.

" What does one king's daughter know about another king's barber?" said the princess.

At this moment the real barber presented himself, and humbly begged the king's pardon for having deceived him.

" But who are you ? " roared the king. "Are you a barber or a thief ? "

"I am the youngest son of a marquess," answered the youth, "a barber by trade, and affianced to the daughter of the King of Castille."

Then the princess stepped forward and explained everything to the king, who was so interested with what he heard, that the princess and the barber had to tell the tale over and over again to him. Then he said—

"I have been shaved by the King of Castille's daughter, and I have courted his barber. I will not be again deceived. They shall now be man and wife for ever."

This was the wise King of Leon.

THE COBBLER OF BURGOS.

NOT far from the Garden of the Widows, in Burgos, lived a cobbler who was so poor that he had not even smiled for many years. Every day he saw the widow ladies pass his small shop on the way to and from the garden; but in their bereavement it would not have been considered correct for them to have bestowed a glance on him, and they required all the money they could scrape together, after making ample provision for their comfort—which, as ladies, they did not neglect—to pay for Masses for the repose of the souls of their husbands, according to the doctrines of the faith which was pinned on to them in childhood.

The priests, however, would sometimes bestow their blessing on Sancho the cobbler; but beyond words he got nothing from the comforters of the widows and of the orphans.

Some of the great families would have their

boots soled by him ; but being very great and rich people, they demanded long credit, so that he was heard to say that a rich man's money was almost as scarce as virtue.

Now, one night, when he was about to close his shop, a lovely young widow lady pushed her way by him into the shop, and sitting on the only chair in the room, she bid him close the door immediately, as she had something to say to him in confidence.

Being a true Spaniard, he showed no surprise, but obeyed orders, and stood before the young widow lady, who, after looking at him carefully for a minute, implored him to go upstairs and see that the windows were secure and the shutters barred and bolted.

This done, he again stood before her, when she showed signs of fear, and requested him to ensure against the doors being burst open by piling what furniture he had against them and against the shutters ; and then, assuring herself that she was safe, she exclaimed—

"Ah, friend Sancho, it is good to beware of evil tongues. I come to you because I know you to be honest and silent. To-night you must sleep on the roof; get out through the skylight, and I will rest here."

To refuse a lady's commands, however singular they may be, is not in the nature of a Spaniard, so Sancho got out through the sky-light, when the young widow began screaming, " Let me out, kind people—let me out!"

The cobbler was now very much afraid of the consequences, especially as the night watch-men were banging against the street door, which they soon forced, knocking all the furniture which had been placed against it into the middle of the room.

When inside, they discovered the lovely young widow, who exclaimed—

"Good men, I am Guiomar, of Torrezon, widow of the noble Pedro de Torrezon, and because my late husband was owing Sancho for soling a pair of boots, I came here to pay the debt; but Sancho would have detained me against my will. He is concealed on the roof of the house, and if you leave me here he will murder me."

Then she naturally fainted and screamed for so long a time that the street was soon full of people who, hearing what had happened, cried out against Sancho.

The watchmen having secured him, he was led before the alcaide, and, being a poor man,

he was sent to prison until such time as Donna
Guiomar should feel disposed to pardon him.

At the end of a year Donna Guiomar
obtained his liberty, but on the condition that
he should forthwith proceed to Rome and do
penance, which was to count for the benefit of
her deceased husband.

This act of piety on her part was very much
approved of by the priests, who required of
Sancho that during the whole of his pilgrimage
there he should not shave, nor have his hair
nor his nails cut. He was, furthermore, to
wear a suit of horse-hair cloth next to his skin,
and was to subsist solely on onions, garlic, maize
bread, and pure water.

But liberty is so sweet that Sancho did not
mind his hard fare, and he went on his way to
Rome repeating penitential prayers, while his
hair and beard grew until his head and face
were nearly hidden.

Arrived at Rome, the people wondered much
to see such a strange-looking being; but when
he opened his mouth to inquire his way to
St. Peter's, so strong was the smell of onions
and garlic that the people, accustomed as they
were to these vegetables, could not stand against
it, and as Sancho spoke in a foreign tongue

they could not have understood him very easily.

At last he met a priest who was kind enough to listen to him, and he said he would be allowed audience of the Pope next morning with other pilgrims, but that meantime he had better confess what his fault had been.

Sancho recounted all about the lovely young widow, and the priest very properly admonished him for having dared to frighten a lady whose anxiety respecting her deceased husband was quite enough of sorrow without having it added to by being forcibly detained by a cobbler.

"It is a pity," said the worthy priest, "that you were not handed over to the inquisitorial brothers, for they would have burned you before you were allowed to import the odour of all the fields of Spanish onions and garlic into the Eternal City. It is a sign of the bad times that are approaching when errant cobblers are allowed to vitiate the precincts of St. Peter's with their pestilential breath. To-morrow you will be regaled with a view—mind, only a view —of his holiness's toe, and then you must depart this city."

Sancho recognized the truth of what the good priest said, and, having refreshed himself with some more onions and a glass of water, he lay down to sleep behind one of the large stone pillars and slept until next morning, when the large bell of the cathedral awoke him. He then hurried in to the presence of the Pope, nor had he much difficulty in so doing, for the other pilgrims were glad to get out of his way. Bowing low before the golden chair, he exclaimed—

"One weary soul, though cobbler he by trade,
　　Comes here to seek a pardon for his sin ;
Most holy father, ere the daylight fade,
　　　　Oh, let me in !

" From sunny Spain, where runs the Arlanzon,
　　To thee, oh, father, come I now to crave
That thou wilt raise Don Pedro Torrezon
　　　　From restless grave,

" And to his widow him restore again.
　　This done, dismiss me to my home in peace,
To be thy servant as a priest in Spain,
　　　　And faith increase."

To which the Pope replied—

" We smelt thee from afar, oh, son of Spain ;
　　We know thy errand, and we grant thy prayer.
Where onions shed their perfume, son, remain,
　　　　Thy presence spare.

"Yes, spare us all thy Spanish odours strong ;
Return unto thy country, Sancho—go ;
And as a blessing on thy journey long,
Stoop, kiss our toe."

And when Sancho got back to Burgos he
was met by Don Pedro de Torrezon, who, half
in anger and half in sorrow, exclaimed—

"Good Sancho, I would spend eternity
Surrounded by the pains of purgat'ry,
Than be restored unto this mortal life,
Where purgat'ry is but the name for wife."

BARBARA, THE GRAZIER'S WIFE.

WHEN Spain was fortunately in possession of the enlightened Moors a spirit
of chivalry pervaded all classes, which degene-
rated after the departure of Boabdil from
Granada.

The Moorish blood permeated the veins of
the majority of the Spaniards; but a religious
despotism completely subdued the minds of
all, and Spain, under the yoke of the Jesuits,
became a land more famed for its *autos da fé*
than for its progress in the fine arts and
sciences, which, to a very great extent, were
ignored.

Some there were, however, in whom the
blood of the Moors was stronger than the faith
in their new religion, which, however good in
the abstract, was most pernicious in its consequences.

It has been the abuse, not the use, of the

Christian religion which has made of the Spaniard what his conqueror, the Moor, would have most loathed.

In the province of Galliza is situated the village of Porrinho, lying in a beautiful valley, and surrounded by meadow-land and fields of maize.

Here lived the merry grazier, Sebastian de las Cabras, famous for his encounters with wolves, but looked down upon by his neighbours because it was known that he was descended from the Moors.

In all the village there was not a man could handle the quarter-staff like Sebastian, and so correct was his aim that, with a sling, he would at a hundred yards hurl a stone and hit a bull between the eyes, and so kill it.

With his knife he was equally skilful, for he could use the blade to pick up the oil from his plate instead of licking it up with a spoon, or, in a quarrel, make it find a sheath in the leg or arm of a rival.

Now, this Sebastian, with all his ingenuity and merriment, had, like most men, a grievance; but, unlike most men's grievances, his was against the good St. Vincent, whose patched-up body (some of it, having decayed, being filled

up with wax) is entombed in different cathe-
drals throughout Spain and Portugal, each
cathedral professing to possess the veritable
body of the veritable saint.

But in this plurality of St. Vincent there is
nothing singular; for did they not fill three
large ships with the eye-teeth of good St.
James of Compostella when they were written
for from Rome, and did not the Pope declare
them all genuine teeth ?

Spain, in her religious fanaticism, is no more
like other countries than Sebastian de las
Cabras was like other men.

St. Vincent, be it known, is worshipped in
the Peninsula as the guardian saint against that
horrible scourge, small-pox.

In Galliza it is declared all diseases and
misfortunes in life were produced in order that
there should be patron saints; and this is just
as true as the saying in Leon, that wheat was
produced so that there might be stomachs.

Sebastian de las Cabras cared neither for the
saints nor for the sayings; he feared neither
the law nor the evil one ; but he quailed before
his wife, D. Barbara, whose beauty, like that of
the demolished alcazar at Ecija, was a thing of
the past.

D. Barbara was, however, a woman who made herself respected ; and of all the saints in the calendar there was none for whom she had so great a veneration as St. Vincent, who had saved her when suffering from small-pox.

Not the three wives who got up from their graves in Merida and appeared to the husband to whom they had all been married, produced a more startling effect on that widower than D. Barbara on her husband Sebastian, when she would visit him as he was tending his herds on the mountain sides, for no woman ever had such a tongue. Even the Archbishop of Compostella, in pity to the clergy of his diocese, had ordained that D. Barbara needed no confession. He absolved her from all sin for the love and veneration she had for St. Vincent, but blamed the good saint for the mercy he had shown D. Barbara.

Sebastian de las Cabras had been to the tombs of St. Vincent in Compostella, in Salamanca, Cadiz, Malaga, and Seville, to induce the good saint to undo his good work; but the bodies were inexorable, and Barbara continued to plague him with her tongue, and to mark him with her nails.

Seeing that he could get no relief for his

home troubles from St. Vincent, Sebastian recollected the faith of his fathers, and bethought of applying for advice to an old Moor who lived in the neighbouring village.

To this wise man he therefore went ; and, after explaining matters, he declared that he bore no ill-will to his wife, but rather to the saint, for that it was owing to him that D. Barbara was spared.

"It is a difficult matter," said the Moor, "and one that will require great consideration and prudence before attempting to master it. You Christians make saints to serve you, and because your interests are not all alike you blame the saints for not doing what is obviously impossible. Now, I know that he whom you call St. Vincent loved the tongue of a woman no better than the scimitar of the Saracen, and for this reason did he probably prefer to spare the life of D. Barbara than be importuned by her in his place of rest."

"What, then, would you advise me to do, for with D. Barbara I can no longer live ? "

"There are St. Nicholas, St. Tiburtius, St. Bartholomew, and others who equally fear the noise of a woman's tongue ; but little St. Francis died stone-deaf, and being naturally of an envious disposition, nothing would please him better than to revenge himself on his colleagues by foisting D. Barbara on to them."

" But if little St. Francis be deaf, how shall I make him hear my complaint ? " demanded Sebastian.

" Thou art no true Catholic if thou knowest not the weakness of the saints in general, but of their keepers here on earth in particular. Thou mayest shout thyself deaf, dance, and jump, but they may not hear thee ; but if thou showest them the bright yellow gold thou wilt be heard and understood, even if thou hadst not a voice, and wert as dumb as thou wouldst wish D. Barbara to be," answered the Moor.

" I will away, then, to the market and sell some of my finest beasts, and the money which I receive for them will I gladly bestow on little St. Francis," said Sebastian.

The oxen were sold, and Sebastian hurried away with the money to the shrine of little St. Francis ; and after devoutly praying, he proceeded to count out the gold pieces one by one ; and great was his joy when he noticed the saint commence to move, open his eyes, stretch out his hands, and declare that Sebastian's petition should be granted.

That very night when Sebastian and his wife were in bed, and the latter was delivering a lengthy lecture on the coarseness and want of breeding in snoring when a lady was speaking, little St. Francis appeared at the bedside with a mirror in his hand.

"Barbara," said the saint, "thy virtues are known to us, and as a reward we have decreed that thou shalt be restored to youth and beauty, which thou shalt thyself behold when looking into this mirror ; but beware no angry or vain words pass thy lips, for then will thy lack of modesty be punished by hideous old age and infirmity, therefore, beware !" And saying this, he left the now happy pair—Barbara admiring herself in the mirror by the light of a cruse, and Sebastian enjoying that unbroken sleep which he had not known for years.

The mirror never passed out of D. Barbara's possession, and was never known to leave her hand until her frame, gradually tired out by want of rest, succumbed to the fascination of little St. Francis's gift and the wisdom of the friendly Moor.

THE WATCHFUL SERVANT.

THERE was once a prince who was going to visit his lady-love, the only daughter of a neighbouring king; and as he required the services of an attendant, he sent for his barber, who was known in the town for his very good behaviour, as well as for his eccentric ways.

"Pablo," said the prince, "I want you to go with me to Granada to assist me on my journey. I will reward you handsomely, and you shall lack for nothing in the way of food. But you must don my livery, salute me in the fashion of Spain, hold my stirrup when I mount, and do everything that is required of a servant. Above all, you must not let me oversleep myself, for otherwise I shall be late in arriving at Granada."

"Sir," answered the barber, "I will be as true to you as the dog was to St. Dominic.

When you are sleeping I will be on guard, and when you are awake I will see that no harm approaches you ; but I beg you not to be annoyed with me if, in trying to be of service to you, I do unwillingly cause you any annoyance."

"Good Pablo," continued the prince, "say no more, but return to your shop, pack up your linen, and come here as soon as you can this evening. If I am in bed when you arrive, you will know that it is because I must get up to-morrow morning by five o'clock, and see to it that you let me not sleep beyond that time."

Pablo hurried home, packed up his few articles of underclothing, and then proceeded to the principal wine tavern to tell his friends of his good fortune. They were all so pleased to hear of Pablo's good luck that they drank to his health, and he returned the compliment so often that at last the wine was beginning to tell on him, so he bid his friends good-bye and left, saying to himself, "I must wake his highness at five o'clock." This he kept repeating so often that he had arrived at the large courtyard of the palace before he was aware of it.

The prince's bedroom looked into the court-yard, and Pablo saw by the dim light that was burning in the room that the prince had retired to rest.

Afraid lest the prince should think he had forgotten all about awaking him, and that he might therefore be keeping awake, Pablo seized a long cane, with which he tapped at the window of the prince, and kept on tapping until the prince appeared, and opened the window, shouting out—

"Who is there? Who wants me?"

"It is I," said Pablo. "I have not forgotten your orders; to-morrow morning I will wake your highness at five."

"Very good, Pablo; but let me sleep awhile, or else I shall be tired to-morrow."

As soon as the prince had disappeared Pablo commenced thinking over all the princes of whom he had heard, and he had become so interested in the subject that when he heard the cock crow, imagining it was daybreak, he again seized the cane and tapped loudly at the window.

The prince again lifted up the sash, and cried out—

"Who is it? What do you want? Let me sleep, or else I shall be tired to-morrow."

"Sir," exclaimed the barber, "the cock

has already crowed, and it must be time to rise."

"You are mistaken," replied the prince, "for it is only half an hour ago since you woke me; but I am not annoyed with you."

Pablo was now sorely troubled in his mind because he thought he might give offence to the prince, and so he kept revolving in his mind all that his mother had told him about the anger of princes, and how much it was to be dreaded. This thought so perplexed him that he resolved on putting an end to the life of the cock that had caused the mistake. He therefore proceeded to the poultry-yard close by, and seeing the offender surrounded by the hens, he made a rush at him, which set all the fowls cackling as if a fox had broken in.

The prince, hearing the noise, hurried to the window, and in a loud voice inquired what the noise was all about.

"Sir," said Pablo, "I was but trying to punish the disturber of your rest. I have got hold of him now, and your highness may go to sleep without further care, as I will not forget to waken you."

"But," continued the prince, "if you waken me again before it is time, I will most decidedly punish you." Saying which he again retired to rest.

"Since the days when cocks crew in the Holy Land they have always brought sorrow into this world," inwardly ejaculated Pablo. "His proper place is in the pan, and that is where he should go if I had my way."

All at once Pablo commenced to feel very sleepy, so he walked up and down the yard to keep awake; but becoming drowsy he sank on the ground, and was soon so fast asleep that he dreamt a nigger prince was attacking him, which made him scream so terribly that it woke, not only the prince, but also all the dogs in the neighbourhood.

The prince again rushed to the window, and hearing Pablo scream out, "Don't murder me, I will give you all!" hurried down into the yard, and seeing how matters stood bestowed such a hearty kick on Pablo that he jumped up.

The frightened barber beholding the prince near to him, took to his heels, and ran home as fast as he could.

When he had got into bed he began regretting that he had run away from the prince's service, so he got up again, saying to himself, "The prince shall have a sharper spur than I could ever buckle on;" and, proceeding to the principal door of the palace, he wrote the following words with chalk, " Pablo has gone before your highness to court the Princess of Granada himself."

This had the desired effect, for when the prince arose in the morning and was leaving the palace alone, he read the words, and they caused him to be so jealous that he performed the distance in half the time he would otherwise have taken.

Pablo after that used to say that "a jealous man on horseback is first cousin to a flash of lightning and to a true Spaniard."

SILVER BELLS.

I T was in a lovely pine-wood that little Mirabella wandered lonely and hungry. The
sand under her feet was very cool, and the
tufted pine-trees sheltered her from the fierce
rays of the sun.

Through an avenue of tall but bare pine-
trees she could see the big sea, which she
looked upon for the first time. Faint and
hungry as she was, she could not help wishing
to be nearer the waves; but she recollected
what her father had once told her, that little
children should be careful not to go too near
the sea when they are alone.

Her father, however, was dead. He was
King of the Silver Isles, and for his goodness
had been loved by all his subjects. Mirabella
was his only child; and her mother having
married again, she wanted to get rid of Mirabella, so that her little boy Gliglu might inherit

the crown. So she ordered one of her servants to lead Mirabella into the pine-wood far away and leave her there, hoping the wolves would find her and eat her.

When Mirabella was born, her aunt, who was a fairy, gave her a silver bell, which she tied around the child's neck with a fairy chain that could not be broken. In vain did her mother try to take it from her; no scissors could cut through it, and her strength could not break it, so that wherever Mirabella went the silver bell tinkled merrily.

Now, it so happened that on the second night on which she was out the silver bell tinkled so loudly, that a wolf who happened to be near, hearing it, approached her and said—

"Silver bell, silver bell, do not fear;
To obey you, Mirabella, I am here."

At first the little girl was very much afraid, because she had heard of the cruelty of wolves; but when he repeated the words, she said—

"Dear Mr. Wolf, if you would be so kind as to bring me my mamma, I would be *so* obliged."

Off ran the wolf without saying another word, and Mirabella commenced jumping for

joy, causing her silver bell to tinkle more than
ever. A fox, hearing it, came up to her and
said—

> "Silver bell, silver bell, do not fear ;
> To obey you, Mirabella, I am here."

Then she said, " Oh, dear Mr. Fox, I am *so*
hungry! I wish you would bring me something
to eat."

Off went the fox, and in a short time he
returned with a roast fowl, bread, a plate,
knife, and fork, all nicely placed in a basket.
On the top of these things was a clean white
cloth, which she spread on the ground, and on
which she placed her dinner. She was indeed
thankful to the fox for his kindness, and patted
his head, which made him wag his thick brush.
She enjoyed her dinner very much ; but she
was very thirsty. She thought she would try
tinkling her bell, and no sooner had she done
so than she heard the tinkling of another bell
in the distance, coming nearer and nearer
to her. She stood on tiptoe, and she saw a
stream of water flowing towards her, on which
floated a pretty canoe. When it got up to her
it stopped, and inside the canoe was a silver
mug; but on the bows of the canoe was hanging
a silver bell just like her own.

"Silver bell, silver bell, do not fear;
  When thy mother comes, step in here."

So sang the canoe; but she could not understand why she should get into the canoe if her mother came, because she loved her mother, and thought her mother loved her. Anyhow she took hold of the mug, and, filling it with water, drank it up. Water, which is always the most refreshing of all drinks, was what the tired little girl most needed, and as her father had brought her up very carefully and properly, she had never tasted anything stronger; but her thirst made her enjoy the water more than she ever had.

Suddenly she heard some one screaming for help, and the screams came nearer and nearer to her. She turned round and saw the wolf bearing her mother on his back, and however much she tried to get off she could not, because the wolf threatened to bite her. Springing up to Mirabella's side, the wolf said—

"Silver bell, silver bell, do not fear;
  To obey you, Mirabella, I am here."

The wicked mother now jumped off his back, and commenced scolding Mirabella for having sent for her. She said that as soon as she got back to the palace she would make a law

that all the wolves should be killed, and that if
Mirabella ever dared return she should be
smothered. The poor little girl felt very
miserable, and was afraid that her mother
might kill her, so she stepped into the canoe,
and said—

> " Bear me where my father dwells,
> Tinkle, tinkle, silver bells."

The stream continued to flow, and as the
canoe moved on she saw her mother turned
into a cork-tree, and she bid good-bye to the
wolf and the fox. On sped the boat, and it
soon neared the big sea ; but Mirabella felt no
fear, for the stream struck out across the ocean,
and the waves did not come near her. For
three days and nights the silver bells tinkled
and the canoe sped on ; and when the morning
of the fourth day came, she saw that they were
approaching a beautiful island, on which were
growing many palm-trees, which are called
sacred palms. The grass was far greener than
any she had ever seen, for the sun was more
brilliant, but not so fierce, and when the canoe
touched the shore—oh, joy !—she saw her dear
father.

> " Silver bell, silver bell, do not fear ;
> To protect thee, Mirabella, I am here."

She was *so* pleased to see her father again and to hear him speak. It was so nice to be loved, to be cared for, to be spoken kindly to. Everything seemed to welcome her; the boughs of the sacred palms waved in the summer breeze, and the humming-birds, flitting about, seemed like precious stones set in a glorious blaze of light. Her father was not changed very much; he looked somewhat younger and stronger, and as he lifted her in his arms his face seemed handsomer and his voice more welcome. She felt no pang of sorrow, she had no fears, for she was in her father's arms, to which the fairy silver bells had led her.

Farther up in the island she saw groups of other children running to meet her, all with silver bells around their necks; and some there were among them whom she had known in the Silver Islands. These had been playmates of hers, but had left before her.

So periods of light sped on, in which joy was her companion, when, looking into a deep but very clear pond, she saw a gnarled cork-tree, which seemed to have been struck by lightning. Long did she stand there gazing into it wondering where she had seen that tree. All at once she spied a canoe passing close by the tree, in which stood a young man, whom she recognized as her step-brother Gliglu. He seemed to cast a sorrowful look at the tree, and then she recollected the fate of her mother. At this moment her silver bell fell off, and, sinking into the pond, it went down—down, until it reached the tree, and, tinkling, said—

"Take thy shape again, O queen!"

Then Mirabella saw her mother step into the canoe; and tinkling bells in a short space of time told her that others dear and near to her had arrived, and, running down to the shore, she cried out—

"Silver bells, O mother, wait you here,
Nought but joy with father, nought to fear."

KING ROBIN.

THERE was once a little boy called Sigli, who, I am sorry to say, took great pleasure in catching and killing little birds. His father was a notorious robber, so it was not surprising that Sigli gave way to acts of cruelty. His mother died when he was little more than a year old, and he did not know any other relation. In the north of Portugal, bands of robbers used to frequent the roads, and some of them lived in strong castles, and had a large retinue of followers. In time of war these robber-chiefs would side with the king's party, because after the war was over they received large grants of land for the assistance they had rendered the sovereign. Sometimes when the neighbouring kings of Spain invaded Portugal, these robbers proved of great advantage in repelling the invaders; but in following up their victories they would despoil all the churches in the enemy's country of the gold and silver idols, which the priests had caused to be made in order to get the ignorant peasantry to make offerings of money, corn, and oil, in exchange for which the priests, in the name of the idols, offered all those who gave, pardon of their sins.

Now, Sigli's father had on many occasions robbed gold and silver idols, and had murdered a few brethren of the Holy Inquisition, who, in their turn, were well known for the wicked deeds they had committed, such as burning Christian men and women who did not, and could not, profess the popish faith. But in course of time the Jesuits, for so they were called, made common cause against these robbers, and either put them to death, or obliged them to leave off robbing churches and take to cheating the peasantry.

Sigli, as I said before, was a very cruel boy, and he was the terror of all the birds and beasts. He would lay traps for them, and when he had caught them he would take pleasure in tormenting them, which clearly proved that he was not a Christian, nor possessed of any refinement. But he took more pleasure in catching Robin-redbreasts

I

than in anything else, and for this purpose he used bird-lime. He had caught and killed so many that at last King Robin of Birdland issued invitations to all his feathered subjects and to the beasts of the field, asking them to a meeting at which they might discuss the best means of putting Sigli to death, or punishing him in some other way, for the cruelty of which he was guilty towards them.

Among the many who accepted the invitation was an old fox, the first of the Reynards, and when it came to his turn to speak, he said that as Sigli was so fond of catching redbreasts with bird-lime, he (Mr. Reynard) would propose catching Sigli in the same manner; and when caught they might discuss how they should punish him, either by pecking and biting him, or by getting the wolves to eat him. In order to carry out this idea, he suggested that the monkeys should be asked to prepare the bird-lime, which they might use with safety by oiling their hands, and then gradually make a man of bird-lime close to the obber chief's castle. Sigli would probably take it for some poor man, and hit it, and then he would not be able to get away.

This idea was accepted by all in general, and

by Mrs. Queen Bee in particular, who owed
Sigli and his father a grudge for destroying her
hive; and the monkeys cheerfully set to work,
while King Robin watched the putting together
of the figure, and was very useful in giving it
most of the artistic merit it possessed when
finished. The making took one whole night, and
next morning, almost opposite the castle, stood
the bird-lime figure about the size of a man.

Sigli, seeing it from his dressing-room window,
and taking it for a beggar, was so enraged
that he ran out without his shoes and stockings,
and, without waiting to look at the man, he
struck at him with his right hand so that it
stuck firmly to the figure.

"Let go," he cried, "or I will kick you!"
And as the figure did not let go he kicked it,
so that his foot was glued. "Let go my foot,"
he cried out, "or I will kick you with the
other;" and, doing so, both his legs were glued
to it. Then he knocked up against the figure,
and the more he did so the more firmly he
was glued.

Then his father, hearing his cries, rushed
out, and said—

"Oh, you bad man! I will squeeze you to
death for hurting my dear Sigli!"

No sooner said than done, and the robber chief was glued on to the bird-lime figure.

The screams of the two attracted the attention of the servants, who, seeing their robber master, as they thought, murdering his little boy, ran away and never came back again.

King Robin was now master of the situation, and he directed ten thousand bees under General Bumble, and another ten thousand wasps under Colonel Hornet, to fall on the robber and cruel Sigli and sting them to death. But this was hardly necessary, as the wriggling of their bodies so fixed them to the figure that they died of suffocation.

Then King Robin ordered the wolves to dig a large grave, into which the monkeys rolled Sigli, his father, and the bird-lime figure; and after covering it up, they all took charge of the castle, and lived there for many years undisturbed, acknowledging King Robin as their king; and if the Jesuits did not turn them out, I am certain they are still there.

THE WICKED KING.

THERE was once a king who was so wicked that he would not allow any widows to live in his kingdom, because he was certain that they had caused the death of their husbands; nor would he admit of any fat man or woman, as he was afraid that they would eat up everything in the kingdom.

He was also very proud and arrogant, and if any man happened to be taller than himself, he would give him the choice of being lowered to a proper height by either having his head or his legs cut off.

His subjects were so afraid of him and of his laws, that the married women would not let their husbands go out of their sight, lest any harm should happen to them, and if they turned at all pale, or had broken sleep, or had lost their appetites, they would nurse them night and day. So afraid were they of becoming widows that they always agreed with their husbands on all points, lest by disagreeing they should bring about an attack of indigestion, or something worse that might produce death.

And when their children commenced to grow rapidly, their fears were doubled lest they should become taller than the king; for if they fed them on pudding, which does not promote growth, they incurred the danger of their becoming fat; and if they fed them on meat, so as to make them lean, they would probably grow tall.

It very soon became evident that there were more hunchbacks in that country than in any other; for as soon as the children were approaching the forbidden height, their parents would suspend heavy weights from their shoulders, so that their backs became rounded and eventually humped.

The young men, when they were at an age to marry, found it very difficult to get any woman to have them, because they were afraid of becoming widows, and also because so many of the men were humpbacked.

But, notwithstanding the king's wickedness, it was admitted by the married men that their condition had considerably improved.

There was a wide road made round the cities and towns, on which all who were inclined to be stout, both men and women, would run until they were out of breath, and jump over hurdles; and there were so many of these people that the revenues of the Church commenced to suffer, owing to the decreased demand for "bulls," as they willingly imposed long fasts on themselves.

Now, in the chief city of this country there was a very wise man, well versed in the law and in concocting drugs, for he was the public executioner and the chemist of the place. To him, therefore, went a deputation of the people to lay their grievances before him; and after the spokesman had finished what he had to say, the executioner looked very wise, and, after considering awhile, he said—

" Our king's predecessor was held to be just and generous because he allowed every man to retain a fifth of his produce for the maintenance of his family, and the tax he imposed on this fifth part was always readily paid." Here he touched the edge of his sharp axe and smiled; and the deputation exclaimed—

" Quite right; so it was."

" Now, the present king," continued the wise

man, again feeling the edge of his axe, "has magnanimously increased your loyal tribute to him by one part in a hundred of the produce of the land, and yet you are not satisfied!"

"The king's generosity we all feel," said the deputation; "but, if we may be allowed to express an opinion to you, sir, we would——"

"Certainly you may," interrupted the man of drugs, running his hand quickly over the axe—"certainly you may; why should you not?"

By this time the chief spokesman had got behind the others, and it was very evident that the members of the deputation were becoming aware that the logic of the executioner was too sharp for them.

Seeing that they were all silent, the executioner went on to say that the king had, in his opinion, been extremely considerate; for he had, by the law against widows, contributed to the happiness and long life of the husbands; and, by enacting that no man should exceed a certain height or stoutness, they had economized in many ways, for they ate less, and their clothes would cost them less. In fact, he saw no reason for dissatisfaction; but as they had come to him as a deputation, he felt it to be his duty to place their supposed grievances before the king, and he, the executioner, felt certain that the king would reply to them in a suitable manner. And having said this he raised the axe to the light to see that there was no notch on the edge, which caused the deputation to tremble most violently, and to assure the executioner that they were perfectly satisfied, and desired to withdraw.

The executioner, however, would not allow them to retire—for the grievances of a people should not be withheld from the king's ear; but the members of the deputation became so frightened that they made their escape through the windows as fast as they could. And when the king heard all about it he remarked that "Folly had entered with dignity by the door, and Wisdom had unceremoniously escaped through the window."

THE PALACE OF THE ENCHANTED MOORS.

OVERLOOKING the river Douro, close to Freixo, are some huge rocks, situated on the brink of an almost perpendicular eminence. To this spot do congregate, so it is reported, the souls of unbaptized children, who make the midnight hour hideous with their shrieks when the tempest is hurrying down through the valley and over the snow-capped hills. When the wind is at its highest do these souls of the lost utter their weird shrieks, so nigh akin unto the howling of the wind that only the neighbouring villagers pretend to be able to distinguish between the clamouring voices of the unbaptized and the howling caused by the fitful gusts of the wintry blast as it rushes impetuously among the rocks and down the precipices.

On such nights will the farmer's wife light

the tapers around the image of good St. Laurence, patron of the winds, and calling her
household around her, the following verses are
intoned—

> " Good St. Laurence, keep us free
> From the sin of heresy ;
> Lull the angry winds to rest,
> Still be thou our honoured guest,
>   By our fathers prized.

> " Drive all goblins from our door,
> Those whom Heaven doth ignore—
> Witches, demons, bogeys all,
> May they sink and may they fall
>   With the unbaptized."

At times it takes longer to appease the wrath
of St. Laurence than at others ; but with daylight the courage of the worshippers revives,
and the souls of the unbaptized seek rest,
although the winds may continue to howl.

Many centuries ago the palace of the now
enchanted Moors at Freixo was the glory of
the place. Although considerably smaller, it
was after the style of the Alhambra, at Granada ;
but it was held in almost greater esteem than
the principal residence of the Moorish kings,
for in a magnificent stable was lodged the ass
on which the prophet Mohamed was supposed

to have ascended to Paradise. It seems that the chosen quadruped, unaccustomed to the pastures of the Mohamedan Paradise, had escaped, and descended on earth close to the palace, or alcazar, at Freixo, where he was found one morning by the dwellers when they were on their way to the mosque.

He was a fine specimen of an ass, and worthy of the Mohamedan creed. Tradition hints at a miller having laid claim to him ; but as he could offer no proofs why the ass should not have been in Paradise, and seeing that the ass was as white as the prophet's, the miller was ordered to look for his donkey elsewhere, as this was the ass of the prophet.

How long this favoured quadruped lived is not recorded, but no doubts have been raised as to his eventual demise ; and he, too, was heard braying furiously from his resting-place when the winds blew high.

But few vestiges are now left of this once splendid alcazar. Time defied its ornamental turrets and richly chased walls, and levelled them with the ground. Only the surrounding rocks have remained, and with them many traditions. These the inhabitants of the district have preserved intact, or maybe added to their interest by investing them with a semblance to truth which renders them all the more worthy of preservation, as being stepping-stones carrying us back to a long past.

But even where such doubtful lore holds the people in awe, a few may be found who, although rejecting that part of the tradition which is evidently but the fruit of a fertile imagination, or of religious fanaticism, recognize in these legends the preservation of a still unwritten history, to whose identification with facts the ruins of many a Moslem building of rare architectural beauty attest.

And if, after many a sanguinary fight, the Cross was victorious over the Crescent, the Christian population of the Iberic Peninsula must admit that the faint vestiges of beauty in their architecture of to-day have an Arabic origin ; that to their Moorish conquerors they owe much of the daring and endurance which characterized the generation of great navigators, as also to them was due the introduction of many of the useful arts and sciences.

The traveller will now look in vain for the alcazar of El Rachid at Freixo. The mighty rocks alone mark the spot, and naught remains of art to please the eye. Traditionary lore may interest him, but he must be ready to listen to it with all the additions which a gross superstition can alone invent or believe.

Here, then, is it recorded that Al Rachid held a Christian maiden captive for many years. That she was as good as she was beautiful goes without further remark. Maria das Dores, for so she is named by her chroniclers, was one of those splendid women worthy to be the mothers of that succeeding generation of heroes who overthrew the Moors on the plains of Ourique.

Maria was the daughter of a very wealthy farmer who resided close to the mouth of the river Minho. It was her duty to work with the farm labourers in the field, and she would mingle her sweet voice with theirs when singing hymns to the Virgin as they plied their hoes.

Often had Al Rachid seen her at work from his hiding-place in a neighbouring forest. He loved the maiden, although he had reason to believe she was a Christian; but he knew that she had given her love to another, and could, therefore, not be his unless he took her by force.

One day, at vesper-time, she did not return

to the farm with the labourers. Search was made for her everywhere, but she could not be found. Then it was imagined she might be in conversation with her lover; but, on inquiry, he had not seen her.

Mounted parties scoured the country all around, but in vain; she had not been seen, and there was no doubt entertained but that she had been lured into the forest, and become the captive of Al Rachid.

But, then, nobody had seen the Moorish chief that day. True; but the Moors were enchanters, and it was known that they could make subterranean passages which closed behind them so as to prevent their being pursued.

The wise woman of the district was therefore called into requisition, and she, having consulted the astrolabe and made a fire of pine needles, discovered the direction in which the fugitives were going. Mounting their horses, and led by the wise woman, who bestrode a splendid white mule, they galloped off, and after two days' hard riding they distinctly heard the sound of a horse's hoofs, but they could not see the horse.

Then they knew that Al Rachid was making use of the enchanted passage which they could

not hope to find, and they had to content themselves with following the sound until they came
within sight of Al Rachid's palace.

They were now in the enemy's country, and
with their little force they could not successfully
besiege the palace, so, much against their will,
they returned home.

There was only one means of rescuing the
captive maiden, and this would take time.   No
Christian man or woman could gain admittance
to the enchanted passage, and no Moslem could
be found willing to attempt the rescue.   Therefore they hit upon a plan of securing the services
of a heretic.   A child had been born in the
village, and him, it was resolved, they should
not baptize.   When old enough, he should be
entrusted with the task of rescue, and being
unbaptized he would gain admittance to all the
enchanted places.

Years rolled by, and the youth had attained
the age of thirteen, when he was informed of
the mission on which it was intended to send
him.   Being of a daring disposition, he courted
danger, and buckling on his sword, and bearing
his shield, he left the farmer's house ; and,
accompanied by the wise woman, he directed
his steps to the forest.   When the two had

reached an old oak-tree, the wise woman repeated the following words three times—

> " Here stands an unbaptized
> To thread the subterranean way ; "

and then she knocked with her staff three times on the ground, which opened, and the youthful heretic boldly descended, the earth closing above him. Before him was a magnificent display of jewels studding the walls on each side, whose brilliancy at first dazzled him. Getting more accustomed to the strong light, he discovered a coal-black horse, fully caparisoned, standing by his side, as if ready for him to mount ; but he was not to be tempted, for he would rather trust to his legs than to a strange horse. Then when he had walked some distance he came to a river, on which there was a boat rowed by six lovely maidens, who asked him to get in, and they would row him across. But he would not be tempted, and he boldly waded the stream and crossed over. Having proceeded a little further, however, he heard the piteous cry of a child, and, hastening forward, he saw a lovely little boy, dressed in the Oriental fashion, who besought him, with tears in his eyes, to carry him a little way, for he was very tired and had still a long

K

way to go. He could not refuse him, and, stooping slightly, raised him in his arms; but no sooner had he done so, than this little boy turned into a giant, who, twining his arms around the heretic's neck, would have strangled him, but that, being unbaptized, he could not be killed. After many attempts to strangle the intruder the giant relaxed his hold, and as suddenly disappeared.

The heretic, after a time, came to a standstill, for he was confronted by total darkness. Nothing daunted, however, he drew his sword and hit out, so that the blade, striking against the sides of the passage, caused the jewels to emit sparks, and these lit up thousands of lamps. In the distance he saw two enormous tigers, each having two heads. They seemed to be ready to tear him to pieces, but, on observing him advance sword in hand, they ran away.

At the end of the third day he had walked so quickly that he stood before the secret entrance to the alcazar of Al Rachid. The ponderous gates were wide open, but he could not enter because of an enormous frog that blocked up the way, and emitted flames of fire from its mouth and eyes. Do what he could, there was no getting near the hideous creature.

He had recourse to stratagem, and, pretending not to be afraid of the animal, he threw his sword over the frog's back, exclaiming, " Take that ; I fear thee not ! "

The frog, turning to get hold of the sword, offered an opportunity to the heretic of jumping on its back, which he did, and, digging his spurs into its sides, he obliged it to advance, when, as it passed by his sword, he dexterously picked it up, and was not at all particular how he used it about the creature's head.

The more he struck at the frog, the more fierce were the flames of fire it emitted ; and Al Rachid, hearing the noise, hurried to the entrance to see what was the matter, when he found himself enveloped in flames which the heretic forced the frog to throw out until the cruel Moor was completely burned.

Then at one stroke he cut off the animal's head, and at the same moment the castle vanished, and where it had previously stood the heretic found Maria, the farmer's daughter, who was overjoyed at her deliverance.

The two wended their way back to their native village, where great rejoicings awaited them ; and seeing that the services of the heretic would in all probability no longer be required, he was baptized with as little delay as possible, and for the rescue he had effected the rich farmer amply rewarded him, while the Church accorded him plenary absolution for his past heresy.

THE SEVEN PIGEONS.

ON a deserted part of the rock-bound Cantabrian coast, a poor fisherman, named Pedro, discovered a lovely maiden, magnificently dressed, combing her long jet-black hair with a golden comb studded with diamonds.

It was still early morning, and the sun had not attained its greatest power; and as the tide was at its lowest, an innumerable number of ponds were formed by the rocks which, for a distance of half a mile, were left bare by the receding sea.

Seated near to one of these ponds, and cooling her feet in the water, sat this lovely maiden; and she was so intent on performing her toilet that she did not perceive Pedro, who, thinking she was a mermaid, and might therefore cast a spell over him, hid behind a ledge of rocks, and was able to see and hear her without being seen.

Pedro heard her singing the following words—

> " I am daughter of a king
>   Who rules in Aragon,
> My messengers they bring
>   Me food to live upon.
> My father thinks me dead ;
>   My death he did ordain,
> For that I would not wed
>   A wicked knight of Spain.
> But those whom he did send
>   To kill me in this place,
> My youth they did befriend,
>   But cruel is my case."

" Is it even so," said Pedro to himself, " that this lovely maiden is the daughter of a king ? If I render her assistance I may incur great danger, and if I leave her to die it will be a crying shame ; what, then, am I to do ? "

As he was thus pondering in his mind, he heard a flapping of wings, and, looking in the direction whence the noise came, he saw a pair of perfectly white pigeons bearing a small basket between them, strung on a thin golden bar, which they held at each end between their beaks.

Descending, they deposited the basket by the side of the princess, who caressed them most tenderly, and then took from the basket some articles of food which she greedily ate (for she had not eaten since the previous morning), and after having finished the contents she again sang—

"I am daughter of a king,
　Who thinks that I am dead ;
Here on this beach I sing,
　By pigeons I am fed.
Thank you, my pretty birds,
　Who are so kind to me.
But what avail my words?
　Oh, I a bird would be !"

This wish was no sooner uttered than Pedro, much to his astonishment, saw that the lovely princess had been turned into a white swan, with a small gold crown on the top of its head.

Expanding her wings, she gradually rose high above him, attended by the pigeons, and all three flew out to sea ; when suddenly Pedro observed a magnificent ship not far from the coast, whose deck was of burnished gold, and her sides of ivory fastened with golden nails. The ropes were of thread of silver, and the sails of white silk, while the masts and yards were made of the finest sandal-wood.

To the ship the three birds flew, and no sooner did they alight on the deck than

Pedro observed that they were three beautiful maidens.

The princess sat on a richly ornamented chair, and the other two maidens on velvet cushions embroidered in gold at her feet.

Over them was spread a superb awning to shelter them from the rays of the sun, and the vessel glided about over the vast expanse of water, now in one direction, now in another, as if the breeze blew to suit the sails.

Pedro was so astonished at what he saw that at last he got frightened, and, being young and nimble, he soon lost sight of the ship; but at every pace he seemed to hear a voice saying, " Run not away, future king of Aragon ! "

Pedro continued running till he left the beach far behind, and was now in the pine-forest ; nor did he stop till he was in the densest part, when, for very fatigue, he threw himself on the ground, and then he distinctly heard a voice say, " Pedro, you are destined to be King of Aragon ; but tell no one."

Not till then had he discovered that he was no longer dressed in fisherman's attire, but that his clothes were of the finest cloth fringed with gold lace.

Pedro, on seeing this, said, " I am enchanted.
That princess is indeed a mermaid, and has cast
a spell over me. I am undone, my eyes deceive
me, and what I take for so much grandeur is
but a deception." Saying which, he started to
his feet, and hurried towards his village as fast
as his legs would carry him.

Arrived at the fishing hamlet, all his old
companions paid him such deference that he
tried to get out of their way, thinking they did
but laugh at him, and, arriving at the door of
his widowed mother's cottage, he ran into the
kitchen. His mother happened to be frying
some fish, and when she saw a grand gentleman
enter the apartment she took the pan off the
fire, and, bowing low, said, " My noble sir, this
house is too humble for such as you ; allow me
to conduct you to his reverence's house, for
there you will find accommodation more suited
to your high estate."

Pedro would have replied to his mother, and
sought to kiss her hand and ask her blessing,
after the custom of the country; but, on attempting to speak, his tongue hung out of his mouth,
and he made so strange a noise and so gesticu-
lated that his mother was glad to get out of
the house, followed, however, by her son and

a large crowd of villagers who had congregated to see the grand stranger.

As soon as it was known throughout the village of the arrival of the grand stranger the church bells pealed, and the parish priest mingled with the crowd desirous of seeing the new arrival; but as soon as Pedro commenced gesticulating as before, the priest and all the rest of the people were much frightened, for they thought that he was dangerously mad.

Pedro, noticing this, sorrowfully turned away from his native village and took the high-road to the next town.

As he was going along, thinking of his present trouble, he observed a wide gate made of gold, opening into a beautiful garden, into which he hesitated not to enter; for he recollected what the wise woman of the village had once told him—that "grand clothes beget respect."

"Open wide those gates, O worker midst the flowers," exclaimed Pedro to an old gardener (for he had now recovered his speech). "I come in cloth of gold to speak unto my love."

"Sir," replied the old man, "you may always enter here, for you are D. Pedro of Aragon, I well can see."

" What very high balconies, a hundred feet in height!" exclaimed Pedro. " Tell me, good old man, does the princess ever come there ? "

" To those balconies so high, to feel the cooling breeze," replied the gardener, "the princess comes there every evening alone."

" Should she ask you," continued Pedro, "who I am, tell her that I am your son come from a distant land, and I will help you to water the pinks."

At her usual time the princess came to her favourite balcony, and seeing Pedro watering the flowers, she beckoned to him, saying—

"O waterer of the pinks, come a little nearer and speak to me."

" Is it true that you desire to speak to me ?" inquired Pedro of the princess.

" No mirror bright ever reflected the truth more correctly than the words I uttered conveyed my desire," answered the princess.

" Here, then, you have me," said Pedro. " Order me as your slave ; but give me, for I am thirsty, a small ewer of water."

The princess poured some water into a silver goblet, and having handed it to Pedro, he exclaimed—

" And in this mirror bright of crystal water

pure, which does reflect thy form, I quench my heart's deep thirst."

"You see yonder palace at the end of the garden," said the princess to Pedro. "Well, in that palace you will be lodged for the night; but should you ever tell any one what you see there, you will put yourself in danger and cause me great trouble."

Pedro promised to keep secret whatever he might see that night, and bidding "good night" to the princess, he hastened to the palace which the princess had pointed out to him, and, having entered it, he walked through the marble passage, which seemed to be interminable. On each side of him were rows of majestic columns, surmounted by gold capitals, and now and again he thought he saw the forms of lovely young maidens flitting among the columns.

Just as he was approaching a richly carved fountain surrounded by sacred palms, a maiden of surprising beauty seemed to be addressing a Moor in most impassioned tones, as if claiming his indulgence; but when Pedro got up to them he discovered that both were the work of the statuary.

At every step the surroundings became more magnificent, and the carved ceiling was of such

exquisite workmanship that it seemed rather
the work of the loom, being so like the finest
lace, than of the sculptor.

At last he arrived at the end of this avenue
of columns, and noticing a door in front of him,
he opened it, and found himself standing on a
marble quay, against which the sea waves were
washing.

Scanning the vast expanse of water before
him, he observed approaching him the same
beautiful ship he had seen in the morning.

When the ship came alongside the quay, a
sailor sprung on shore, and made her fast by
a golden cable; then, addressing Pedro, he
said—

"I am glad you have not kept us waiting,
for our royal mistress is very wishful to consult
you, as one of her favourite doves has broken
its right wing, and if you cannot cure it, the
princess will die of starvation."

Pedro made no reply, but stepped on board
the ship, which soon got under way, and within
a short time they were approaching the coast
he knew so well.

Having landed, Pedro saw the princess
seated on the sand, nursing one of her white
pigeons.

"Pedro of Aragon," the princess exclaimed, "a stranger dared to enter my royal father's garden, and in assisting to water the pinks he trod on the wing of my favourite pigeon, and he has broken it."

"Señora," replied Pedro, "the intruder did probably seek you, and had no idea of hurting the lovely bird."

"That matters not," continued the princess, "for my principal supporter is wounded, and you must cure her. Cut out my heart, and steep this bird in my warm blood, and when I am dead throw my body into the sea."

"How can I kill one so lovely?" asked Pedro. "I would rather die myself than hurt you!"

"Then you do not care for me, or else you would do as I bid you," answered the princess.

"Princess, I cannot and will not kill you; but I will do anything else you bid me," said Pedro.

"Well, then, since you will not kill me, I order you to take this pigeon back with you; for I know it was you who walked in my father's garden to-day," continued the princess. "And to-morrow evening, when you see that princess whom you saw to-day, you must kill her, and let her blood fall over this pretty bird."

Pedro was now in great trouble, for he had promised the princess to do anything she told him to do, except killing her, and he could not break his word; so taking hold of the pigeon very gently, and bidding good-bye to the princess, he again stepped on board the ship, and so depressed was he that he had arrived at the marble quay without being aware of it.

On landing, he retraced his steps through the avenue of pillars, and found himself once more in the garden, where the old gardener was again watering the pinks.

" What very high balconies!" exclaimed Pedro. " Tell me, old gardener of the ancient times, if the princess comes here to-day."

" The princess loves the fresh sea-breeze," answered the old man, "and to-night she will come to the balcony, for her noble lover will be waiting for her."

" And who is the princess's lover?" inquired Pedro.

" If you will help me to water the pinks, I will tell you," said the old man.

Pedro readily acquiesced, and putting down the pigeon where he thought no harm would happen to it, he commenced assisting the gardener to water the pinks.

After a silence of a few minutes the gardener said—

"There were once seven pigeons who said, 'Seven pigeons are we, and with other seven pigeons we might all be mated ; but, as it is, we must remain seven pigeons.'"

"Yes," put in Pedro ; "but I want to know who the princess's lover is."

The old man took no heed of the interruption, and continued—

"There were once seven pigeons who said, 'Seven pigeons are we——'"

"Stop!" cried Pedro ; "I will have no such idle talk. Tell me who this noble lover is, or I will do you an injury."

"Sir," cried the gardener, with a very serious countenance, "there were once seven pigeons who said, 'Seven pigeons are we, and——'"

"Take your watering-can," shouted Pedro in disgust ; "I will not listen to your nonsense !"

"And yet there were once seven pigeons who said, 'Seven pigeons are we ;' and now the last of them is gone, for the noble lover has been false to his trust," exclaimed the old man, looking very cunningly at Pedro.

At these words Pedro looked towards the place where he had placed the pigeon, and it was no longer there.

Seized with a fit of fury, he was about to lay hands on the gardener, when, to his astonishment, he found that he was also gone.

" I am undone," cried the unhappy Pedro ; "and now I shall not see the princess again." Saying which he fainted away, and might probably have remained there some time, but that he heard a voice saying, in a jocular manner—

" There were once seven pigeons who said, ' Seven pigeons are we, and——' "

Pedro started to his feet, and close to him was standing the princess whom he had previously seen in the balcony.

" Why do you thus tease me, princess ? " said Pedro. " I want to hear no more about the seven horrid pigeons."

" Don Pedro de Aragon," answered the princess, " I must tell you that the old gardener to whom you spoke is a magician, and he has possessed himself of the last means I had of regaining my liberty, for I am under his power. Is it not true that you came here with the purpose of killing me ? "

" I was under a vow to do so," replied Pedro ;

"but I cannot kill you, although I would rather slay you, fair princess, than do you a more grievous injury."

"Go back, then, to the unhappy lady whom you left on the sea-shore, and tell her that you have been false to your promises," said the princess.

"How sorry I am," exclaimed Pedro, "that I was ever destined to be King of Aragon! When I was a poor fisherman, I was far happier than I am now!"

"Pedro of Aragon, the moon will be at the full to-night, and you may then rescue me," said the princess, "if you have the courage to meet the wicked magician in this garden at midnight, for then is his power weakest."

"I am prepared for the worst," replied Pedro, "and I fear not your gaoler."

"Well, then," continued the princess, "when the magician sees you he will again tell you about the seven pigeons; but when he has finished, you must tell him that there were once seven wives who had only one husband, and that they are waiting outside to see him. Do as I tell you, and if you are not afraid of his anger, you may be able to free me."

Pedro promised to do as he was told, and

the princess having retired into the palace, Pedro amused himself by walking under the lofty balconies, watching the fire-flies grow brighter as night came on.

Just about midnight the magician was seen watering the pinks, and as soon as he perceived Pedro he said—

" There were once seven pigeons who said, ' Seven pigeons are we, and with other seven pigeons we might all be mated; but, as it is, we must remain seven pigeons.' "

" Quite so," put in Pedro. " And once upon a time there were seven wives who had only one husband, and they are waiting outside to see him."

The magician, at these words, lost all control over his temper; but Pedro heeded him not, rather did he endeavour to increase his rage by repeating all about the seven wives.

" I am undone !" cried the magician; " but if · you will induce the spirits of my seven wives to again seek the grave, I will give you what you want, and that is the princess."

" Give me the princess first," answered Pedro, "and then I will free you of your wives."

" Take her, then," said the magician; "here she is. And forget not what you have promised me, for I may tell you in confidence that a man with seven wives cannot play the magician."

Pedro hurried away with the princess ; and after they had been married and crowned, the princess, who was now queen, one day said to him—

" Pedro, the magician who held me captive from you was Rank, and therefore were the balconies so high. When you saw me on the beach fed by pigeons, it was that you should know my power; on the shore I was attended by winged messengers, and on the sea I sailed about at pleasure."

" But what about the wounded pigeon ? " asked Pedro.

" Recollect, Pedro, what you said to me in the garden," answered the princess—" that you would rather slay me than do me a more grievous injury. That poor pigeon with its broken wing could no more hope to soar aloft than an injured woman to mix with her former associates."

" And what about the seven wives who were waiting outside, and who so frightened the old magician, Rank ? " continued Pedro.

" They are the seven deadly sins, who would each have a tongue for itself, and yet without tongues are enough to frighten Rank," answered the princess.

" And who am I, then," asked Pedro, " to be so exalted now ? "

" You are the wise man who strove to do his best, yet tried not to exalt himself above his position," sweetly answered the princess.

" So that the magician Rank has unwillingly raised the poor fisherman to be king," whispered Pedro.

" Not Rank alone, but much more so thy own worth."

LADY CLARE.

TRANSLATION.

LADY CLARE was in her garden over-looking the sea. It was a summer's day, and the many coloured butterflies flitted about under the trees and among the sweet smelling flowers.

Lady Clare was combing her golden tresses with an ivory comb, seated on a crimson velvet cushion. She looked towards the sea, and she saw a gallant fleet making for the land.

He who was in command stepped on shore. He was a belted knight, but his features could not be seen as his vizor was down.

Approaching Lady Clare, he saluted her, and she thus addressed him—

" Hast thou, noble knight, seen my husband, who bid me good-bye many years ago when he sailed for the Holy Land ? "

" I know not thy husband, fair lady. By what should I know him ? "

" He took his white charger with its golden trappings with him," answered Lady Clare. " On his lance he bore a red pennon ; a tress of my hair served him for a belt, from which hung his sword. But if thou hast not seen him, Knight of the Cross, then woe be to me, lonely widow, for I have three daughters, and they are all unmarried."

" I am a soldier," continued the knight ; " war is my employment. But what wouldst thou give, fair lady, to have thy husband near ? "

" I would give thee more money than thou couldst count, as well as the roof of my house, which is made of gold and ivory," answered Lady Clare.

" I care not for gold nor money ; they are of no use to me, for I am a soldier and engaged in war, and I never saw thy husband. But what wouldst thou give, fair lady, to have him here ? " inquired the knight.

" I would give thee my jewels, which cannot be weighed nor measured ; I would give thee my golden loom and my distaff of burnished silver," said Lady Clare.

" I neither wish for gold nor for silver : with

steel is my hand better acquainted, for I am a warrior, and I never saw thy husband. But what wouldst thou give to have him near thee ? " cried the knight.

" I would let thee choose one of my daughters; they are as fair as the moon, or as the sun when rising," urged Lady Clare.

" I do not want thy daughters ; they may not marry me, for I am a soldier and engaged in warfare, and I never cast eyes on thy husband. But what wouldst thou give to have thy own knight here ? " exclaimed the warrior.

" I cannot give thee more, nor hast thou more to ask of me," replied Lady Clare.

" Thou hast still more to give, for thou hast not yet offered thyself, fair lady," said the knight.

" A belted knight who dare so speak deserves to be dragged around my garden, tied to the tails of my horses. Come hither, my vassals, and punish this rude soldier!" exclaimed Lady Clare.

" Do not call for thy vassals, for they are mine also," said the knight; "and do not be angry with me, for I have already kissed thee."

" Then thou art surely my brave lord," said

Lady Clare; "but how wilt thou prove thyself?"

"By the golden ring with seven gems which
I divided with thee when I left," answered the
knight. "Here is my half; where is thine?"

"My daughters," cried the Lady Clare,
"bring hither my half of the ring, for your
father is here to claim it! But, oh, my husband,
joy at seeing thee again had nigh made thee
a widower."

GOOD ST. JAMES, AND THE MERRY BARBER OF COMPOSTELLA.

JUST close to the cathedral of Compostella lived a barber whose real name was Pedro Moreno, but who was better known by that of El Macho, "the mule," because he was so stubborn that if he happened to be playing the guitar, he would not leave off though a dozen customers were waiting to be shaved. But in Spain a barber also applies leeches, draws teeth, and extracts corns, so that it was very annoying for a man who was suffering from tooth-ache, and wanted his tooth taken out or stopped, to have to wait until the barber had finished playing on the guitar.

He was also a soothsayer, and could repeat the whole of the prophetical *Buena Dicha* by heart. He was, in fact, the most useful man in Compostella, and had cultivated the art of shaving the face and head from the commence-

ment which consists in watching the flies when
standing close to the master who is showing off
his skill on a customer, to being able to play
the guitar with such proficiency that, holding
the neck in his left hand and pressing the cords
with the fingers, he shall, by thumping the
instrument on the big toe of his left foot, cause
it to vibrate the air of the immortal *Cachucha*
or the *Bolero*, while with his right hand he
plays the castanets.

A barber may have his brass chin-basins,
which hang outside the door, burnished every
day; his fly-catcher renovated every month; his
bottles containing leeches nice and clean ; and
he may know all the scandal of the town, which
is decidedly a part of his duty; but if he cannot
play the guitar and the castanets at the same
time—which he can only do by calling the big
toe of his left foot into requisition—he must not
be considered a barber of the first class. He
may do for shaving poor priests and water-
carriers ; but he may not shave an abbot, nor
an archbishop, still less a grandee of Spain, who
may sit before the king with his hat on.

In other countries the position of a barber is
somewhat less important than it used to be
when cleanliness required of a man that he

should appear at early mass on the Sunday well shaved; but in Spain, cleanliness of the face is a great recommendation, for a rough chin never earned kisses. Therefore is a barber still held in great respect in the land of the Cid; and although Don Pedro Moreno was known by the name of " El Macho," no one would have dared address him thus.

One day the archbishop called on El Macho to request of him to come and look at the image of St. James in the cathedral, to whom the edifice is dedicated, because this miraculous figure, who had wrought so many miracles, had, strange to say, commenced letting his beard grow, much to the astonishment of all the priesthood and of the common people, and to the dismay of several knights who had been knighted at the altar of St. James, because in those days knights did not use beards.

The barber, seeing the archbishop enter his house, advanced, knelt, and kissed his ring; and, knowing on what errand he was come, he was so solicitous of securing the archbishop's favour, that he put aside his guitar, and respectfully awaited the prelate's commands.

The archbishop having informed Pedro of the state of St. James's chin, proceeded to inform him that it had been decided, at a meeting of the clergy, to entrust the shaving of the saint to him, Pedro Moreno ; but that, as this growth of hair was most exceptional, seeing that the image was of wood, it was probable that the usual process of shaving might not be sufficient.

" And you are quite right, most excellent sir, in your supposition," exclaimed the barber; "for unless I obtain some of the holy water in which the good saint was baptized, and a piece of the soap with which Judas Iscariot greased the rope with which he hanged himself, it will be useless to try and shave him, for the hair will grow as fast as it is taken off."

" But that is impossible," answered the archbishop ; " for we do not even know where the good saint was baptized ; and as for the soap last used by the arch-traitor, I should not be astonished to hear that Satan had taken it away with him when he came to fetch Judas. No, good Pedro ; you must help me out of this difficulty in some other manner."

" Then we must do with St. James of Compostella what the men of Burgos did with their alcaide, who persisted in getting drunk when he ought to have been getting sober. They got another alcaide as much like the other as possible, excepting that he was not a *borracho*. We must get another St. James like this one, but without a beard, and the people will be none the wiser."

"But," whispered the venerable archbishop, "what are we to do without our real, own, good, sweet St. James, whose miracles have been the means of restoring so many erring ones to the fold, and bringing in so much money to the Church ? How can we replace him ? And then, again, where can we hide him ?"

"All this can be arranged very easily," answered El Macho. "Any St. James will perform the same miracles, for the people have faith in him. It is the same with me ; the hidalgos have faith in me, and therefore believe I am the only man in Compostella that can shave them, although there are many other barbers. It is the people's faith that performs the miracles. As for hiding the saint, I will put him in a box I have got, and lock him up safely."

"Fair sir, I leave the matter in your hands," continued the archbishop ; "but beware lest the people get to hear of it."

And having said this he mounted his mule and rode off.

El Macho went in search of a sculptor, a friend of his, and told him that he wanted an image made exactly like that of St. Iago's in the cathedral, because he had made a vow that should he live single up to the age of fifty, he would endow his parish church in Cordova with a St. James. He pressed his friend to make haste, and told him he would pay him well for his trouble.

At the end of ten days the image was finished and handed over to the barber, who, in the middle of the night, with the assistance of the archbishop, entered the cathedral, took down good St. James, disrobed him of his armour, and having put it on the new St. James, placed him on the altar, and then carried the old image home.

Having locked the door, he proceeded to place the saint in the wooden box, but found out that his legs were too long; so he cut two holes in the side, through which he allowed them to project, and, putting down the lid, locked it.

Next morning, after the first mass was over, the people gave vent to their pleasure at seeing that St. James had a shaven face as formerly; and the barber, who was at the door, gained great praise by informing them that he had been the unworthy means of shaving their saintly patron.

Now, the saint, who heard this from his box, commenced to hit about him, and shouted out—

"Good people, I am St. James with the beard. El Macho is a villain!"

But the people laughed, thinking it was the apprentice who was in the alcova, or inner room, and had not got over the previous night's drinking. So they went their way, laughing at the idea of a beardless boy thinking he was good St. James with the beard.

Matters went on very well with regard to the new St. James, who was not deficient in working such miracles as the people liked to ascribe to him and to believe of him. The belted knights were pleased to find out that the growing of a beard was only a passing fancy of their patron; and as all were satisfied, and the revenues increased, the priests were also well pleased.

Good St. James had been confined within his box for about three months when the day for

his annual procession came round, and great
preparations had been made for the occasion.
Each knight had sent his war-horse fully caparisoned, led by two servants in the livery of the
family, and followed by his shield and spear-
bearers. There were about one hundred and
fifty such chargers which preceded the horse
bearing the image of St. James, who was kept
secure in the saddle by a knight walking on
each side, holding his legs, while another one
followed bearing his banner. Then came the
standard-bearers of the knights, each with a
page richly dressed, and then came the archbishop under the pallio, surrounded by the
dignitaries of the cathedral and minor priests of
the neighbouring villages. All the holy brother-
hoods presented themselves in their different
coloured robes, with their gold and silver
crosses, their richly emblazoned banners; and
in their midst walked little girls dressed up to
imitate angels, while the little boys swung
censers of burning incense. In the rear came
twelve squadrons of cavalry, four batteries of
artillery, and five brigades of infantry, which
had arrived from different garrison towns to
take part in the procession. From every
window scarlet damask drapery hung, as well

M

as from the balconies where the lovely daughters of Spain in all their holiday grandeur appeared, fanning themselves gracefully—which art they have cultivated to the detriment of conversation, which to them is still an art little attended to.

The streets through which the procession had to pass were strewn with flowers, especially fleurs-de-lis, and crowds had congregated on the pavements.

El Macho had given his apprentice a half-holiday, and was standing outside his house, speaking to some customers, when he suddenly heard a great noise, and turning round he saw that good St. James in the box was running towards the cathedral from which the procession was emerging. Peals of laughter and shouts of " El cajon " (" The box ") were taken up by the multitude ; but, fortunately for El Macho, they did not see from which house the box on legs had come.

Not waiting for admittance, and knocking over the sentries at the door, the saint in the box made straight for the archbishop, who, knowing what it was, quietly walked into the vestry, followed by St. James, and locked the door.

Then he undid the box, and beheld good St. James with a three months' beard on his chin, who shouted—

" Have me shaved, good archbishop! Let me take my place in this grand cavalcade, and I promise not to grow a beard again."

The archbishop enjoined silence ; and calling for one of his acolytes, he ordered him to stop the procession for half an hour, to have the horse carrying the other St. James led into the enclosed yard, and send for the barber, El Macho. This having been done, the barber was ordered to shave the saint and put on his armour, which the other one was wearing. This did not take long ; but even so the people wondered at what had happened, which, however, they were never to know—not even the mystery of this box on legs—because the archbishop issued a pastoral granting plenary absolution to all such as should not ask him any questions, and excommunication to all such as should find out.

Once again on horseback, and surrounded by his faithful knights, St. James received the homage of the vulgar crowds and of the lovely ladies, and returned to his old place on the altar.

That he did not relish being locked up in the box for three months is proved by the fact that when, on three or four occasions, his vanity got the better of him, and the archbishop thought he saw signs of letting his beard grow, it was quite sufficient to show him the big box for him to withdraw the obnoxious bristles.

The new St. James was presented to the parish church at Cordova by El Macho, and his vow having been thus accomplished, he married the archbishop's niece, gave up business, and died shortly after.

ELVIRA, THE SAINTED PRINCESS.

WAMBA was king of the Goths, who inhabited the northern part of Lusitania. He was one of the bravest kings that ever reigned, and the walls of his palace still stand as evidence of the skill with which he studied to improve his capital. But although he was wise, he was not a good man, and his bravery in war was not tempered by mercy. Like all his predecessors, he was cruel to his victims, and was more feared than loved.

Wamba had but one daughter, Elvira, whose mother was a princess of the Moorish family reigning in Andalusia. She was so beautiful and so good, that she contributed in no small degree in rendering her father's reign famous. Her long hair was of a lovely glossy black; her eyes, of the same dark hue, had all the softness of her race, and it was this very tenderness of look that gave majesty to her appearance.

In those days there were but very few

Christians in Europe. The Crescent of the false prophet had overcome for a time the Cross of the true Saviour. To the teachings of an old man, who in secret worshipped the true God, Elvira owed the first lessons she got of Christianity; and once the good seed was sown, it multiplied.

Wamba did not know that his daughter was a Christian; but he knew that she was very good, and that for her goodness she was very much beloved by all his subjects.

Now, it so happened that in the dungeon of his palace there were many prisoners condemned to death by starvation, and it perplexed the king to know how it was that they continued to live. Every morning he would ask of the gaoler if the prisoners had died, and the answer was that they seemed quite well.

So one day he hid in a nook of the staircase, hoping to find out who fed his prisoners. He had not long to wait, for he soon saw Elvira descending, followed by a young courtier, Alaric, and carrying something in her apron.

Elvira, unknown to her father, had been in the custom of carrying bread to the poor prisoners, and she was assisted in her work of mercy by her lover Alaric.

When she got close to the king, he started out of his hiding-place, and seizing her by the arm, she, in her fright, let fall her apron, out of which fell beautiful roses, into which the bread had been transformed.

Great was the surprise of the king, for he thought she was carrying victuals. Then, in his rage, he said—

" Elvira, thou art in league with the evil one, and thou and thy lover shall die !"

Elvira and Alaric were themselves so astonished at what had taken place, that they could not speak, and allowed themselves to be led away to separate gaols without offering an explanation.

Wamba had it proclaimed that next day his daughter Elvira and her lover Alaric would be burnt in the public square for having dealings with the evil one. Many of his oldest courtiers tried to persuade him that he was too precipitate; but he was not to be moved, and all that night Elvira and Alaric were preparing to meet death.

At the first ray of light Wamba was up, and with his soldiers and executioners hurried to the public square. Elvira and Alaric were led among a strong body of men, and everything was being prepared for burning the lovers, when Elvira's old tutor presented himself before Wamba, and said—

"Know, O king, that thy daughter fears not death, for her comfort is on the Cross, and not on the Crescent. If any one be to blame, I am he, for I instructed her. Let me, then, be burned in her stead."

Wamba gazed fiercely at the old man, and, raising his massive olive staff surmounted by a gold crown, exclaimed—

"Thou shalt also die, but not before thou hast witnessed her sufferings. Thy God is a false God, or if He have power to save all of you, He shall cause this ancient olive staff to grow and throw out green leaves by to-morrow morning, or else you shall all die;" and saying this, he stuck his royal staff into the ground.

Elvira was to be allowed to remain close to the staff, but no one with her; and, so that she might not escape, guards were posted all round the square.

Kneeling at the side of that emblem of authority, which for generations had been wielded by her ancestors, she gave vent to her prayers and tears, and the latter fell so quickly that they moistened the ground; and when morning came, Wamba, on arriving, saw his royal staff growing, a sapling then, but shortly to grow into a tree, even as the Christian faith in its sapling stage was to throw out its spreading branches over the kingdom, till they all became one people, loving but one God.

Wamba caused a church to be built near the spot, which church still exists; and the olive-tree grows by its side, giving the name of Olive-tree to the Square.

Alaric was married to Elvira; and Wamba having been called to the grave of his forefathers, these two reigned conjointly, and appointed the old tutor their counsellor.

THE ENCHANTED MULE.

THERE was once a very merry, but very poor hostler in Salamanca. He was so poor that he had to go about his business in rags; and one day when he was attending on the richly caparisoned mule belonging to the Archbishop of Toledo, he gave vent to his feelings in words.

"Ah," said he, "my father was always called a donkey from the day of his marriage; but would to goodness I were the archbishop's mule! Look at the rich livery he bears; look at his stout sides; see how he drinks up his wine and eats his maize bread! Oh, it would be a merry life, indeed! My father was, they say, an ass, so I would be a mule!"

And then he leant against the manger, and laughed so heartily that the archbishop's mule stopped eating to look at him.

"What ho!" said the mule. "Remember that

my reverend master, being a corpulent man, is somewhat heavy; but if thou wilt change conditions with me, thou need but take hold of both my ears, and, *caramba*, a mule thou shalt be, and that in the service of the Archbishop of Toledo!"

"And that will I," answered Pablo the hostler; "for better be a well-fed mule than a starving hostler." So saying, he seized the mule by the ears, and, looking at him in the face, he was immediately transformed; but, to his surprise, he saw that the quondam mule was changed into a monk. "How now!" cried he. "Wilt thou not bring me some more wine and maize bread, sir monk? Wilt thou not be my hostler?"

But the monk turned away and left the stable, and Pablo then saw that he had made a mistake. But he resolved that as soon as he was led out into the street he would run off to his old mother, and implore her to intercede on his behalf with the patron St. James of Compostella.

When the archbishop had rested, he called for his mule, which was brought out; and, in the absence of the hostler, whom they could not find, one of the attendants was about tightening the girths, when the mule Pablo, seizing the opportunity, bolted away as hard as he could down the road in the direction of his mother's house.

The archbishop thought his mule had gone mad, and as the servants followed it, running, and crying out, "Stop the beast—stop it!" the rabble joined in the chase; but Pablo never stopped till he got to his mother's house.

The old woman was at the door, spinning at her distaff, and as she was very deaf she had not heard the clamour. Pablo, bending over her, tried to kiss her hand, to ask her for her blessing, but his tongue now failed him. So frightened was she at the approach of the animal that she hit him over the head with her distaff, and cried out, "Abernuncio!"

By this time the servants had surrounded him, and were trying to lead him back, but he would not go. He stood on his hind-legs, and then lay down on his side, and rolled in the dust till the scarlet saddle-cloth was spoilt, and then, suddenly rising, rushed into the cottage, and tried to sit on his accustomed chair.

His mother fled the house, and the rabble entered, and so cudgelled Pablo that he was fain to return to the inn; and, after being groomed, he allowed the archbishop to mount him. However, he had not gone far before he exclaimed, "By St. Iago, this mule hath the pace of a camel!" Pablo, not being accustomed to four legs, did not know how to use them, so that he would move his right fore and hind legs together. This caused the archbishop great inconvenience, for, being a corpulent man, it made him roll about on the saddle like the gold ball on the cathedral of Sevilla, when the west wind loosened it, and the east wind blew it down.

Seizing the pommel with both his hands, and raising himself in his shoe stirrups, he looked as if he intended to vault over the head of the mule; and as they were at this moment going through a village, the inhabitants, who had come out to see the archbishop, thought he was about to deliver a sermon. So, surrounding the mule, they uncovered their heads, and knelt awaiting the blessing.

Pablo, forgetting he was a mule, thought the people were doing homage to him, and being of a merry disposition, he gave way to such inward laughter that it brought on a violent fit of coughing, which the faithful—not seeing the face of the archbishop, for they devoutly bent their heads towards the ground—took to be the natural clearing of the throat before speaking.

But the archbishop, who was now becoming seriously frightened, and thinking that the evil one had entered the body of his mule, exclaimed, "Exorciso te—abernuncio!" Then did Pablo sit down on his hind-quarters, so that the archbishop slid off the saddle and rolled on the ground, and another "Abernuncio!" in a deeper tone, brought the devout people to their feet. Pablo at this moment got up, and by so doing completely capsized the venerable archbishop, causing him to turn over on to his head. Full of dust and anger, the prelate started to his feet, and carefully examined his mule to see if he could account for this peculiar behaviour. Sorely grieved did Pablo feel at having caused the good archbishop so much annoyance, and, so as to show his contrition, he went down on his fore-legs, thinking to kneel, which so frightened all the people that they instinctively took shelter behind the archbishop. But he was as much afraid as the rest, and had it not been that they held him by his robes, he would have run away.

"This beats the mule of Merida," cried one, "who ran away with the miller's wife and then regretted the bargain. See, he is craving for pardon."

Pablo the mule rose after kneeling for some time, and, after the fashion of trained animals of this breed, he extended his fore and hind-legs, so as to facilitate the archbishop mounting him, which he soon did, feeling convinced that the mule had intended no harm; but Pablo, regretting his mistake and the loss of time it had caused, set off at a quick amble, which so disconcerted his rider that he had to hold on by the pommel and the crupper; and thus he was hurried out of the village, and the people were done out of the blessing.

The attendants, who were on foot, tried to keep up with Pablo; but this they could not do, owing to his long strides; and not until they were within sight of Toledo did they get up to their master, who, by this time, was out of breath and countenance. They, fearing that the mule might start off again, placed a man on each side holding the reins, and thus did they approach the eastern gate of the city, at which many priests were waiting with the cross and the sword of the archbishop, in order to give him a fitting welcome, according to the rules of the Church. Pablo, seeing the large silver cross, the emblem of Christianity, slack-ened his pace, and when within a few yards of

it, in obedience to what his mother had taught
him as a child, dropped down on his knees,
bending his head to the ground; but this he
did so suddenly, that the archbishop fell off the
saddle on to his neck, and, to break his fall,
caught hold of his servants by their ears, nearly
tearing them off, and causing them also to
tumble.   Thinking that the evil one had seized
them, they struck out right and left, and nearly
stunned their master with the blows and kicks.
Pablo, hoping to retrieve his fortune, started to
his legs with the archbishop clinging round his
neck, and galloped after the two servants with
his mouth open, so that, should he catch them,
he might bite them.   But they, surmising what
he meant, sought refuge among the priests, and
these in their turn made haste to get into a
small chapel close by.

"Our archbishop must have changed mules
with Beelzebub," said a fat priest, "for no
earthly animal would thus treat a prince of the
Church!"

"Ay," continued one of the runaway servants;
"and if his neck had been a foot longer I should
have been dangling in mid-air like the coffin of
the false prophet."

"I never thought to have run so fast again,"

ejaculated a very short and stout priest. " Faith, my legs seemed to grow under me, as our sacristan said after he had been tossed by the abbot's bull."

" But what has become of the archbishop ? " said another. " We must not leave him in his sorry plight."

Saying this, he carefully opened the door of the chapel, and there they saw their prelate swooning on the pavement, and Pablo dashing full tilt among the crowd, trying to wreak his vengeance on as many as he could possibly get hold of.

Having torn the leather breeches of some half-dozen sightseers, and knocked down and trampled on some score of men and women, he rushed out of the city by the same gate, and never stopped till he arrived at the inn where he had been hostler. The master of the inn, thinking that some mishap had befallen the archbishop, made haste to secure the mule ; but as it was already night, he postponed sending off one of his servants till next morning.

Once again at the manger, Pablo had time to consider over the mistake he had made, and he would gladly have undergone any punishment, could he but have regained his former shape.

N

While he was thus musing, he saw the monk approaching, looking very sorrowful indeed.

"Pablo," said he, "how dost thou like being a mule?"

Now, Pablo was cunning, and, not wishing to let the monk know what had happened, he answered—

"As for liking it, I enjoyed carrying the archbishop as much as he liked being carried; but I am not accustomed to such gay trappings and good living, so that I am afraid of injuring my health."

"If that be the case," continued the monk, "hold down thy head, and I will relieve thee of the danger; for, to tell you the truth, I find out that my wife is still living, and she recognized me although I was disguised as a monk. By my faith, I would rather bear my master's harness to the grave than my wife's tongue from morning till night! *Caramba*, I hear her knocking at the door! Dear Pablo, let us again exchange conditions."

And Pablo, when he awoke next morning, was tightly grasping a beam, thinking he was the Archbishop of Toledo clinging on to the mule's neck.

Upwards of 300 Superb Illustrations (some beautifully hand-coloured).

KENSINGTON: PICTURESQUE AND

HISTORICAL. By W. J. LOFTIE, B.A., F.S.A., Author of
"A History of London," &c., &c. Illustrated by W. LUKER, JUN.,
from Original Drawings carefully finished on the spot and engraved
in Paris.

LONDON: FIELD & TUER, THE LEADENHALL PRESS, E.C.

Since the publication of Faulkner's work in 1820, no history
of Kensington pretending to accuracy or completeness has been
produced. This work contains full and descriptive accounts of
the parish of Kensington and the adjoining Palace and Gardens,
with the changes and improvements of the past half-century
or more ; notices of Kensington celebrities and of the great
national institutions which have sprung up at Kensington Gore
and Brompton Park ; and a fund of discursive matter of local
and historical interest. In regard to the very numerous and
absolutely faithful illustrations, two years have been spent by
the artist in making for this work original drawings of old and
modern Kensington. They include artistic exteriors and interiors ; glimpses of Kensington Gardens ; the Palace in which
the Queen was born ; the park ; the people, streets, houses,
churches, and ruins ; and pretty, quaint, and taking "bits" of
Kensington scenery. All the drawings have been engraved in
Paris in the finest possible manner, and the paper on which
they are printed has been specially manufactured of a quality
that will ensure the delicacy of the originals being fully retained.

For the curious, a few PROOF copies of KENSINGTON :
PICTURESQUE AND HISTORICAL, at five guineas, bound in full
morocco, have painted in water-colours on the front, under the
gilt edges of the leaves, a couple of Kensington views, which,
until the leaves are bent back at an angle, will be invisible.

Now if you want some volumes nice,
You'll start at once I'm su-er,
And go and fetch them in a trice,
From Messrs. FIELD AND TUER.—*Punch.*

EXTRACTS FROM

Field & Tuer's List,

ꊧꊫ + 𝕷eadenꊧall + 𝕻ress,

50, *LEADENHALL STREET, E.C.*

Upwards of 300 Superb Illustrations (some beautifully hand-coloured).

KENSINGTON: PICTURESQUE AND
HISTORICAL. By W. J. LOFTIE, B.A., F.S.A., Author of
"A History of London," &c., &c. Illustrated by W. LUKER, JUN.,
from Original Drawings carefully finished on the spot and engraved in
Paris. LONDON: Field & Tuer, The Leadenhall Press, E.C. £2 5s.

Since the publication of Faulkner's work in 1820, no history
of Kensington pretending to accuracy or completeness has been
produced. This sumptuous work contains full and descriptive accounts of the parish of Kensington and the adjoining
Palace and Gardens, with the changes and improvements of the
past half century or more ; notices of Kensington celebrities and
of the great national institutions which have sprung up at
Kensington Gore and Brompton Park ; and a fund of discursive
matter of local and historical interest. In regard to the very
numerous and absolutely faithful illustrations, two years have
been spent by the artist in making for this work original drawings
of old and modern Kensington. They include artistic exteriors
and interiors ; glimpses of Kensington Gardens ; the Palace in
which the Queen was born ; the park ; the people, streets,
houses, churches, and ruins ; and pretty, quaint, and taking
"bits" of Kensington scenery. All the drawings have been
engraved in Paris in the finest possible manner, and the paper
on which they are printed has been specially manufactured of a
quality to ensure the delicacy of the originals being fully
retained.

For the curious a few PROOF copies of KENSINGTON:
PICTURESQUE AND HISTORICAL at five guineas, bound in full
morocco, have painted in water-colours on the front, under the
gilt edges of the leaves, a couple of Kensington views, which,
until the leaves are bent back at an angle, are invisible.

IN THE PRESS.]

THROUGH ENGLAND ON A SIDE-SADDLE IN THE
TIME OF WILLIAM & MARY; being the Diary of CELIA FIENNES. With an explanatory Introduction by The Hon. Mrs. GRIFFITHS. LONDON: Field & Tuer, The Leadenhall Press, E.C.

IN THE PRESS.]

TALES FROM THE LANDS OF NUTS & GRAPES:
(SPANISH & PORTUGUESE FOLKLORE.) BY CHARLES SELLERS. LONDON: Field & Tuer, The Leadenhall Press, E.C.
[Half-a-Crown.

IN THE PRESS.]

THE BAIRNS' ANNUAL (for 1888-9) of Old-Fashioned Tales.
Edited by ALICE CORKRAN. Illustrated with nearly one hundred original wooden blocks and a coloured Frontispiece. Contents:—The Story of Punch and Judy: The Sleeping Beauty in the Wood: The Butterfly's Ball and the Grasshopper's Feast: Little Red Riding Hood: Hop o' my Thumb: Cinderella and her Little Glass Slipper: Gaffer Gray: a Christmas Ditty: The Apple-Pie Alphabet: Dr. Watts's Cradle Hymn: Peter Piper's Practical Principles: A Merry New Song: The Rudiments of Grammar: The Froward Child Properly Corrected: Tom Thumb. LONDON: Field & Tuer, The Leadenhall Press, E.C. [One Shilling.

A delightful *mélange* of the old-fashioned fairy tales that delighted our grand-parents when bairns.

MEN, MAIDENS & MANNERS A HUNDRED YEARS
AGO. By JOHN ASHTON. With thirty-four contemporary illustrations. LONDON: Field & Tuer, The Leadenhall Press, E.C. [One Shilling.

IN THE PRESS.]

HIEROGLYPHIC BIBLE.
Being a careful selection of the most interesting and important passages in the Old and New Testaments. Illustrated with hundreds of Engravings on Wood. LONDON: Field & Tuer, The Leadenhall Press, E.C. [One Shilling.

A facsimile, crowded with the original quaint illustrations, of an edition of the Holy Scriptures which amused and instructed our great grand-fathers and great grand-mothers when little boys and girls.

A LOVER'S LITANIES.
By ERIC MACKAY, Author of "Love Letters of a Violinist" and "Gladys the Singer." LONDON: Field & Tuer, The Leadenhall Press, London, E.C. [Ten-and-Sixpence.

THE BAGLIONI:
A Tragedy. By FAIRFAX L. CARTWRIGHT. LONDON: Field & Tuer, The Leadenhall Press, E.C.
[Three-and-Sixpence.

PEOPLE WE MEET.
By F. RIDEAL. Illustrated by HARRY PARKES. LONDON: Field & Tuer, The Leadenhall Press, E.C. [One Shilling. A limited edition of 100 only, proof copies signed and numbered.
[Five Shillings.

THE DAWN OF THE TWENTIETH CENTURY:
1st January, 1901. LONDON: Field & Tuer, The Leadenhall Press, E.C. [One Shilling.
"Displays an exhaustive knowledge of the diplomatical relations between the different countries of Europe and of history in general."—*Morning Post.*

A SEASON IN EGYPT. By W. M. FLINDERS PETRIE. Illustrated.
LONDON: Field & Tuer, The Leadenhall Press, E.C.
[Twelve Shillings.

A BOOK OF JOUSTS. Edited by JAMES M. LOWRY, Author of
"The Keys at Home," &c. LONDON : Field & Tuer, The Leadenhall
Press, E.C. [One Shilling.
"· · · exceedingly clever humorous verses · · · we have
not often seen a brighter little volume of its kind."—*Manchester
Examiner.*

FIFTY-FIVE GUINEAS REWARD. A Sensational Story. By
FRED. C. MILFORD, Author of "Lost! A Day." Fifth Edition.
LONDON : Field & Tuer, The Leadenhall Press, E.C. [One Shilling.

THE GRIEVANCES BETWEEN AUTHORS AND
PUBLISHERS, being the Report of the Conferences of the Incor-
porated Society of Authors held in Willis's Rooms, in March, 1887
with Additional Matter and Summary. LONDON: Field & Tuer
The Leadenhall Press, E.C. [Two Shillings.

BEAUTY AND THE BEAST. By CHARLES LAMB. With an
Introduction by ANDREW LANG. Illustrated with eight beautiful steel
plates engraved in facsimile from the original edition. LONDON :
Field & Tuer, The Leadenhall Press, E.C. [Three-and-Sixpence.
A charming book of equal interest to children and their elders.

One hundred signed copies only, containing a set of earliest open-
letter proofs of the eight illustrations in red, and a duplicate set in
brown. [Ten-and-Sixpence : raised to Two Guineas.

No. 1.—DAME WIGGINS OF LEE.

No. 2.—THE GAPING WIDE-MOUTHED WADDLING
FROG.

No. 3.—DEBORAH DENT AND HER DONKEY.
Hand-coloured Illustrations. LONDON : Field & Tuer, The Leadenhall Press, E.C. [One Shilling each.

Reprints of the coloured picture books—illustrated from the
original blocks, hand-coloured—used by our grand-mothers when
young. The costumes of adults and of children at their games,
&c., are very quaint and amusing. DAME WIGGINS OF LEE has
met with the strong approval of Mr. Ruskin.

MODERN MEN. By A MODERN MAID. CONTENTS : The Decay
of Courtesy, Our Partners, Our Fellow Boarders, Husbands and
Brothers, The Vanity of Men, Men and Money Matters, Objectionable
Lovers, &c., &c. LONDON : Field & Tuer, The Leadenhall Press,
E.C. [Two Shillings.

A book in which modern men are amusingly abused.

(3)

abcdefghijklmnopqrstuvwxyz

abcdefghijklmnopqrstuvwxyz

abcdefghijklmrstvvwxyz.

abcdefghikmrstuvyz

abcdefgikopxyz

abcdefghijklxyz

ABCD HXYZ

abcdefghijklmnoœxyz

ABEGWW Z

aabcdeefghïjklmnñopxyz

1234567890

Types from

The Leadenhall Press,

50, Leadenhall Street, London, E.C.

THE HENRY IRVING DREAM OF EUGENE ARAM.
By F. Drummond Niblett. LONDON: Field & Tuer, The Leadenhall Press, E.C. [One Shilling.

A clever skit. Both text and illustrations are on a black ground.

THE SEASONS. By James Thomson. With Four Illustrations and extra Portrait printed direct from the original copperplates, engraved in 1792, and an Introductory Note by John Oldcastle. LONDON: Field & Tuer, The Leadenhall Press, E.C. [Sixteen-Pence.

Having no more original copperplates of a suitable character, the publishers regretfully announce that they are unable to further continue this series. The three preceding issues are *Tristram Shandy, Sir Charles Grandison* and *Solomon Gessner*. The four make a handsome and interesting volume.

SYBIL'S DUTCH DOLLS. By F. S. Janet Burne. Profusely Illustrated. LONDON: Field & Tuer, The Leadenhall Press, E.C. [Two-and-Sixpence.

An amusing book, rendered doubly amusing by the very numerous cuts being unmistakably jointed wooden dolls.

EIGHT TALES OF FAIRY-LAND. By Louise Poirez. With "three times eight are twenty-four" illustrations by V. Gertrude Muntz. LONDON: Field & Tuer, The Leadenhall Press, E.C. [Two-and-Sixpence.

A cleverly written and cleverly illustrated set of fairy tales for children.

GRAY'S ELEGY: with Sixteen beautiful Illustrations by Norman Prescott Davies, facsimiled from his original drawings in the possession, and published by the gracious permission of H. R. H. The Princess of Wales. Bound in gold lettered vellum, with broad silken bands and strings. LONDON: Field & Tuer, The Leadenhall Press, E.C. [One Guinea.

" A work of very great beauty."—*Leeds Mercury.*

FLYING LEAVES FROM EAST AND WEST. (Second Edition.) By Emily Pfeiffer, author of "Sonnets," "Gerard's Monument," "Under the Aspens," "The Rhyme of the Lady of the Rock," &c., &c. LONDON: Field & Tuer, The Leadenhall Press, E.C. [Six Shillings.

" The best book written on the American continent."—*Academy.*

SONNETS. (Revised and Enlarged Edition.) By Emily Pfeiffer, author of "Gerard's Monument," "Under the Aspens," "The Rhyme of the Lady of the Rock," "Flying Leaves from East and West," &c., &c. LONDON: Field & Tuer, The Leadenhall Press, E.C. [Six Shillings.

" They are, to our mind, among the finest in the language."
—*Spectator.*

THE SIGNS OF OLD LOMBARD STREET. By F. G. Hilton Price, F.S.A., with Sixty full-page 4to Illustrations by James West. LONDON: Field & Tuer, The Leadenhall Press, E.C. [One Guinea.

HOUSEKEEPING MADE EASY. By a Lady. A simplified method of keeping accounts, arranged to commence from any date. LONDON: Field & Tuer, The Leadenhall Press, E.C. [One Shilling.

1,000 QUAINT CUTS FROM BOOKS OF OTHER DAYS, including Amusing Illustrations from Children's Story Books, Fables, Chap-books, &c., &c.; a Selection of Pictorial Initial Letters and Curious Designs and Ornaments from Original Wooden Blocks belonging to The Leadenhall Press. LONDON: Field & Tuer, The Leadenhall Press, E.C. [Sixteen-Pence. A limited number printed on one side of the paper only at Two-and-Eightpence.
" A wonderful collection of entertaining old wood engravings . . . . any one of these delights is worth the one-and-fourpence." —*Saturday Review.*

(Dedicated by gracious permission to Her Majesty the Queen.)
SONGS OF THE NORTH. (New Edition.) Gathered together from the Highlands and Lowlands of Scotland. Edited by A. C. MACLEOD and HAROLD BOULTON. The Music arranged by MALCOLM LAWSON. Frontispiece "Proud Maisie," by FRED SANDYS. LONDON: Field & Tuer, The Leadenhall Press, E.C. [Twelve-and-Sixpence.
" A book that singers will like to have and the public will be wise to get."—*The Scotsman.*

THE FIRST YEAR OF A SILKEN REIGN (1837-8). By ANDREW W. TUER & CHS. E. FAGAN. With Ten Illustrations from contemporary plates. ". . . proudly arched neck advancing . . uncurbed with silken rein unfelt."—*Anon.*
CONTENTS.—The Accession: Reminiscences: Early Days of the New Reign: Festivities and Public Appearances: The London of the Period: Society of the Period: Coaching: The Dawn of the Railway Era: Sport: Music, Drama, and Amusements: Art and Ceremonial: The Coronation. [Six Shillings. LONDON: Field & Tuer, The Leadenhall Press, E.C.

(Dedicated by gracious permission to Her Majesty the Queen.)
THE FOLLIES AND FASHIONS OF OUR GRAND-FATHERS (1807). Embellished with Thirty-seven whole-page Plates of Ladies' and Gentlemen's Dress (hand-coloured and heightened with gold and silver), Sporting and Coaching Scenes, &c., &c. By ANDREW W. TUER. LONDON: Field & Tuer, The Leadenhall Press, E.C. Large Paper copies, crown 4to, with *earliest impressions* of the plates; 250 only, signed and numbered, at Three Guineas. Demy 8vo copies at Twenty-five Shillings.
" May at any time be confidently dipped into by readers in search of quiet diversion."—*Graphic.*

JOHN BULL AND HIS ISLAND. (Cheap Edition.) Translated from the French by the Author, MAX O'RELL. LONDON: Field & Tuer, The Leadenhall Press, E.C. [One Shilling. Translated into almost every European language, upwards of two hundred thousand copies of "John Bull and his Island" have been disposed of, and this remarkable book is still selling.

A SET OF FOUR HUNTING AND RACING STORIES. By W. B. GILPIN. LONDON: Field & Tuer, The Leadenhall Press, E.C. [Two Shillings.

(7)